THE SECRET OF THE BLACK HOLE

Patrick Moore read his first book on astronomy when he was six, and is now a world-wide authority on the subject. He is Director of the British Astronomical Association Lunar Section, was awarded the OBE in 1968, and is well-known as a television and radio personality – he has presented the BBC television programme "The Sky at Night" for the last twenty years.

He is the author of a variety of books for both adults and children, and his hobbies include cricket, music and chess.

This is his sixth book about Scott Saunders.

Also available in Armada by Patrick Moore

Scott Saunders Space Adventure Series
SPY IN SPACE
PLANET OF FEAR
THE MOON RAIDERS
KILLER COMET
THE TERROR STAR

Patrick Moore

THE SECRET OF THE BLACK HOLE

A Scott Saunders Space Adventure

An Armada Original

The Secret of the Black Hole was first published in the U.K. in Armada in 1980 by Fontana Paperbacks, 14 St. James's Place, London SW1A 1PS.

Printed in Great Britain by
Love & Malcomson Ltd., Brighton Road,
Redhill, Surrey.

CONTENTS

Chapter 1

THE ROBOT

It was early morning on the moon. The sky was inky black, as it always was even in the middle of the long day; without air, there was nothing to spread the sunlight around and make the sky blue. The brilliant earth was there, partly covered with cloud so that not even the main outlines of the seas and continents could be made out. Scott Saunders stared up at it, looking instinctively for England where he had been born and where he had spent the first sixteen years of his life—that is to say, until he had been recruited into the Space Service and had made his home upon the first of the great orbiting stations whirling round the globe. That had been only three years ago, but a great deal had happened to him since then.

"Homesick, by any chance?" drawled Dr. Homer Lang in his strong American accent. "You're a long way out, kid!"

Scott grinned. "Funny, but I don't think of earth as my home any longer," he said. "Give me Station One, any time. Come to that, I don't much like the moon either."

Dr. Lang shrugged. "Everyone has his own ideas, I

guess. I reckon I'm turning into a real moon-man, but I may think again after I've been here a bit longer. I've a whole lot of work to do before I can get back to the States."

Scott turned away from the earth, hanging in the dark sky above him, and gazed around. He and Homer Lang were standing outside one of the huge domes that had been set up on the moon's surface; like the others, it was made of transparent plastic, kept inflated by the pressure of the air inside it, and by now it seemed almost part of the natural landscape. Once inside the airlocks there was no need to wear a helmet or a cumbersome space-suit, and the only strange thing was the lack of weight. The moon's feeble pull of gravity meant that everything seemed to happen in slow motion, though it was by no means uncomfortable. Outside, it was very different. The lack of atmosphere meant that full vacuum-clothing had to be worn all the time, and it was never wise to go far without taking at least one reserve oxygen tank. Scott had had one experience of being stranded with insufficient oxygen, and he had no wish to go through anything of the sort again.

"You're a bit of a mystery to me," said Homer Lang suddenly. "I know you're one of Wainwright's trouble-shooters, but you don't look old enough for the part. What's behind it?"

"No mystery," said Scott. "I can't help looking like a kid; after all, I'm not twenty yet. I don't think I want to get old." He paused. "Do you know Sir Eustace Wainwright?"

"I've met him once or twice. So far as I can remember, he looks rather like a walrus."

Scott chuckled. "I suppose he does. That moustache of his must be the largest in the Solar System! You know he's Chief of Intelligence—so far as Britain is concerned, I mean?" Lang nodded. "Well, I was one of the cadets he picked out to train. I was a bit lucky, I suppose, because I blundered into all sorts of things straight away, and I managed to make myself useful. We got mixed up with Alpha."

"Alpha," repeated Lang slowly. "Yeah, I've heard of that. It's a kind of secret organization, I know, but I haven't heard a lot about it lately. Wasn't there a man called Brand in charge of it?"

"Carl Brand may not be the head man, but he's just about the most dangerous of the lot," said Scott. "I haven't a clue where he is now. He cleared off after the last spot of bother, and nobody's managed to catch up with him. Hallo—something's coming through the inter-com."

He turned up the volume of the small but powerful radio fitted inside his helmet, and at once he heard Nigel Lorrimer's voice. Nigel was his closest friend; the two had been together ever since Scott had made his first trip into space, and the link between them was very strong. "'Lo there," said Nigel. "Receiving me?"

"Loud and clear. What's up?"

"Message from Station One," said Nigel. "I can't quite make out what it means, but I reckon we may have to get back pretty smartly. Are you coming inside?"

"Hold on for a minute or two," said Lang. "I've something to show you. Come and join us, young Nigel. I think you're in for a surprise."

Scott looked across inquiringly, but Lang merely gave a soft chuckle. "It won't be long," he said. "I had a special reason for asking you to come for a stroll. There's a friend of mine I want you to meet."

Scott felt puzzled, but it was clear that Lang did not mean to be drawn. In a few minutes Nigel came out through the airlock, wearing the usual regulation vacuum-suit, and made his way across the rough, crater-pitted plain. This was one of the so-called lunar "seas", which had never contained any water, but had once been filled with molten lava; the nearest big crater was named Wallace, which was why the dome—the latest to be set up on the moon—was known officially as Wallace Base. "Who's your pal?" asked Nigel curiously. "I don't get it."

"You will in a moment. He's not far off," said Lang, again with that dry chuckle. "Robbie's quite a lad, as I think you'll agree. I wanted some specimens of the rock over there, beyond that big mound, so I asked him to go and fetch them. He's on his way back now."

"Robbie?"

"That's what I call him. There he is."

Lang pointed, and Scott and Nigel stared across the plain; the sun was still low over the horizon, and the shadows were long, but the light was brilliant, so that to look at the sun without protective goggles would have been dangerous. Scott squinted. For a few moments he could see nothing, but then he made out a tiny figure walking with a peculiar, uneven stride. "That's him?"

"That's Robbie," agreed Lang, and switched on his main transmitter. "Robbie, this is Homer. Come back to the dome, please."

"Message understood. I am in good order."

Scott gave Nigel a quick look. There was something very odd about that voice; it was not the accent, but the whole tone had an artificial, metallic ring unlike anything he had heard before. "Keep watching," said Lang softly. "You'll soon see what I mean."

The figure was approaching steadily, and Scott strained his eyes. The mysterious Robbie was walking quickly—or, rather, swaying along, and soon he was plainly visible. Suddenly Nigel let out a yell. "Boy! He's—he's not wearing a suit!"

"He doesn't need one," said Lang. "Tough character, our Robbie. I'll get him to tell you all about it."

"But he can't breathe without a helmet—" began Scott, and then broke off. "Wow! I reckon I've got it. What does 'Robbie' mean?"

"You're there," said Lang approvingly. "Yep, you've hit on it. Robbie the Robot . . . I won't say he can carry on a long conversation, but he can talk, he can do as he's told, and he's a right good guy. Say 'hallo', Robbie."

"I greet you," came the flat, metallic voice. "I greet you."

Nigel burst out laughing. "That beats the band. We've all heard of robots, but I've never seen one looking like a man. Did you make him?"

11

Lang nodded. "Well, I admit I had a big hand in it. I did the original designs, and I fixed him up together with my team—you know most of them; they're right here, in Wallace. I've had my fun. We'll go inside, and I'll put Robbie through his paces."

He led the way back into the dome. Scott and Nigel followed him through the airlock, and once safely inside they were glad to strip off their clumsy vacuum clothes. Lang went back into the lock, and seconds later he reappeared, this time with the awkward-looking but efficient figure of the robot. Robbie really was strikingly lifelike. He was made entirely of metal, but Lang had given him human features, and even the joints of his arms and legs did little to spoil the illusion. "How much can he talk?" asked Scott. "You're not going to tell me that he can think for himself?"

"We haven't got as far as that yet," said Lang, and turned as another figure joined them. "You did most of the talk-box, Leif. That's not my line."

Both Scott and Nigel knew Leif Larsen, the Norwegian scientist who had come to the moon soon after the first bases had been set up; his English was so good that his accent was hardly noticeable. "It is an electronic voice, of course, and it has been programmed so that it gives set replies to set questions. Say 'Hallo Robbie', and he'll answer 'I greet you'. Ask him 'Is everything correct?' and he'll give you a truthful reply: 'Yes' if there's nothing wrong, 'No' if there's a malfunction of any sort. If you want to go much further, you have to work out a programme and put it into what

12

I call his brain. That's how we were able to make him go and collect rocks, for instance. Do you like him?"

"I think he's great," said Scott heartily. "Is he the only one?"

"Yes, at the moment. He's our first model—a prototype, if you like. We'll have two or three others by the end of the year, if nothing goes wrong. We're going to find them very useful, I think, and we've had only one real accident so far."

"With Robbie?"

"Yes. It might have been much worse than it was," said Lang, "but I can't find out what caused it, which is a worry. We'd sent Robbie on a long hike to see how far he could go, and of course we were tailing him in a car." Scott knew that 'car' was the usual American name for the special lunar vehicles which were used to cross the moon's rough surface; really they were more like tractors than cars. "We were some way away from him when he suddenly froze up. Our motors did the same, and I didn't like it one little bit, because we were at least ten miles from Base. The radio was no good, either. It lasted for about an hour, and then—bing!— no more problem. That was when I called up Reggie Vale."

"I heard about that," said Scott thoughtfully. It was generally realized that Dr. Reginald Fordyce Vale, known commonly as 'Scruff' because of his wild untidiness, was the most brilliant scientist on either the earth or the moon; generally he preferred to stay on Station One, but he was no stranger to the lunar surface, and Scott would never forget that nightmare

13

experience of a year earlier, when one of the original domes had collapsed. "That's really why we came, as you know. Reggie had some ideas he wanted to pass on to you, but he didn't give us any details."

"I'm not sure whether they help much," said Leif Larsen. "I don't believe the trouble was due to Robbie, or to us. There has been some strange interference over the last two or three weeks, and it seems to be getting worse. It comes from outside."

"Alpha?" asked Nigel shrewdly.

Lang shrugged. "Could be, I suppose, but—well, we haven't enough to go on. I've half a mind to come across to the Station and talk to Vale myself. He won't say much over the radio for some reason or other, and I reckon he's keeping something back. What was the message that came through while we were out there?"

"It was from Wainwright," said Larsen. "You're to call him up. I don't think it's urgent, but you'd better do as you're told. You'll have plenty of time to look at Robbie later."

Wallace Base was not large; only about a dozen scientists worked there, and only Lang and Larsen had stayed for any length of time. The main control room was of the usual kind, with the familiar radio and television equipment. Vale had helped in building it, together with Thor Eiriksson, the Icelandic boy who had become such a firm friend of Scott and Nigel. Scott went across to the transmitter. "All right for me to call up?"

Lang nodded. "Of course. I guess you know the set-up as well as anyone."

Scott settled down, and switched on the transmitter; the television screen glowed, and Scott spoke into the microphone. "Scott Saunders calling Station One. Do you read me?"

There was a flicker, and then a well-known face came into focus. Sir Eustace Wainwright's vast moustaches seemed to stretch right across the screen, and he really did have the look of a friendly walrus. "Ah! I thought it must be you, my dear fellow. I take it that you've been introduced to Robbie?"

Scott grinned. "I'll say! You never told us about him!"

"I didn't want to spoil Homer's little surprise," said Sir Eustace, with a soft chuckle. "Still, I think it's time for you and Nigel to come home, if you don't mind. There are some rather peculiar things going on, and I have a nasty hunch that we may be in for a bit of trouble."

Scott looked up sharply; he knew that Sir Eustace's hunches were generally very near the mark. "What kind of trouble?"

"I wish I knew. I'm very old and stupid, as you know, and I'm probably barking up the wrong tree. Put it down to senile decay if you like, but—"

Sir Eustace broke off, and Scott leaned forward. Something was wrong. The picture on the screen tilted crazily, and then went blank; after a few seconds Sir Eustace's voice came through again, but the distortion was so great that no words could be made out. Nigel jumped forward by Scott's side. "What is it?" he breathed. "For Pete's sake, what's happening?"

Homer Lang was already operating the reserve television equipment. In a matter of moments the huge, ungainly form of Station One came into view, but it was not steady; it was weaving and shuddering as though being hit with a giant hammer, and Scott let out a shout of alarm. "Look there. Can you hear me? Scott Saunders to Station One—"

There was a pause that seemed endless. Then, slowly, the rocking movement of the Station slowed down, and Sir Eustace could be heard again. "Very nasty. That was the worst yet. Scott!"

"Yes?"

"There is trouble ahead. I was right," said Sir Eustace in a crisp tone quite unlike his usual banter. "No, I can't tell you whether it's our friend Carl Brand or not. I don't know, and neither does Reggie. You'd better stay where you are while we sort it out—"

"Not likely," broke in Nigel. "I reckon we'd rather come over."

Sir Eustace's image on the screen was almost normal now. "I thought you'd say that. Very well. I won't try to stop you, but be on your guard. Call up every ten minutes, and let me know if you look like running into danger. Get moving!"

Chapter 2

SPACE-WRECK

Travel to and from the moon was nothing new to either Scott or Nigel. Both had made the journey at least a dozen times, and both were good pilots; Sir Eustace had once said that Scott was probably the most skilful flyer in the whole of the space-service, and the Chief of Intelligence never said anything that he did not mean. The very first lunar journey, by Apollo 11 so long before, had taken two and a half days; by now it was a matter of a few hours, thanks mainly to the new power-drives that Vale had pioneered. Checking the ferry-rocket took some time, because there was so much that could go wrong, and a moment's carelessness could mean disaster, but at last all was ready, and Scott strapped himself down. "Right?"

Scott made a routine call to Base Control. "Permission to take off, please."

Homer Lang answered. "O.K. for take-off. Good luck. Be seeing you!"

The motors roared, and the ferry lifted off from the lunar surface with the usual deceptive slowness. Blasting away from the moon was much easier than leaving the earth, because the pull of gravity was so much less, and the feeling of pressure as the speed built up was not nearly so violent. In less than three minutes they were in free fall, and all sensation of "weight" vanished. Scott checked the course. "All right so far. What do you reckon it can be?"

"Search me, pal," grunted Nigel. "Reggie's screen doesn't seem to have done the trick this time." In their earlier battles with Carl Brand and the mysterious Alpha organization, Vale had developed a protective shield around the Station which had saved it from being blown to pieces by a nuclear bomb launched against it, but this was something different. "I'd better see if they can hear us."

He tuned in, and sent out a preliminary call. At once Thor Eiriksson replied. "Thor here. Anything to report?"

"Seems normal at present," said Nigel. "Gee! that looked rocky. Must have caused a lot of damage."

"Quite a bit here and there. The telescope in the observatory has been knocked around, and poor old Juan Santos is trying to fix it." Santos and his fellow-astronomer, Paul Monk, were permanent residents of Station One; they were popular with everybody, even if they did have a well-earned reputation of being the worst pilots in the Solar System. "No casualties, luckily."

"Any idea what caused it?"

"All we really know is that it was outside interference of some kind. Station Three has been hit, too; Gregory Voronov is over here, and he's been telling us

18

that the same thing happened on Three a few hours ago. Reggie's getting some ideas, I think."

"Alpha?"

"I doubt it. This doesn't seem to be deliberate," said Thor slowly, "but so far we haven't been able to track it down, so we can't be sure. Better keep your receiver switched on. Let me know if you want a course check; I'll be standing by."

For some time there were no alarms. Nigel called regularly, and Thor answered; the moon shrank from a vast plain into a globe hanging in space, and the earth swelled in size until it filled much of the sky. The hours passed uneventfully. First Scott and then Nigel snatched some sleep; while the ferry-rocket was on course and in free fall there was very little to do except keep a constant check. Then, suddenly, Scott called out. "Nigel. Wake up."

"What's the matter?" asked Nigel sleepily, rubbing his eyes. "Anything up?"

"Not sure, but the instruments have gone crazy. Look at this."

Nigel swung himself across the cramped cabin, and stared. "You're right, pal. I reckon something's being beamed on to us. If we—"

He broke off abruptly as the ferry-rocket gave a violent lurch. Neither of the two boys had strapped down in their couches, and the jolt took them completely by surprise; Nigel cannoned into Scott, and the two thudded against the wall with a blow which knocked the breath out of Scott's body. Lurch—jolt! Again the ferry shuddered, and Scott gave a painful gasp; somehow or other he managed to swing back to the controls, but for some seconds there was nothing he could do to stop the pitching and heaving. "Hold on," he roared. "I can't steady her!"

Slowly the violent jolting died away, and the ferry settled down. There was still a slight vibration, but the main attack seemed to be over, and Nigel straightened up. "Gee! That was pretty bad. We'd better make sure the pressure's holding up. Are you all right?"

"I'm O.K.," said Scott thickly. "Air-pressure normal, but the instruments are still crazy. Try a call."

Nigel was already operating the radio transmitter, but with no result. "Dead as mutton," he muttered, and stared hopelessly at the small but powerful radio set. "Hallo. Nigel Lorrimer to Station One. Do you read me? Answer!"

Nothing came through but a loud, unsteady hiss, and Nigel shrugged. "No go. That means we can't get any course corrections either. If the motors have been scuppered too, we're in trouble."

The same thought had occurred to Scott, and he did not like it. They were still thousands of miles from the earth, and the space-stations were only a few hundreds of miles above ground level. Navigation in the quarter-million-mile gap between earth and moon was not normally difficult, but without engine power there was real danger. When he switched on to give a brief thrust nothing happened, and he set his jaw firmly. "Motors dead. I'll check up to see where we'll end up if we can't change course. That bang may have chucked us out of the orbit I'd worked out."

Again and again Nigel called on the radio, but still there was no answer, and he began to fear that the transmitter had been put out of action permanently. What could have caused it? There was no sign of anything nearby; so far as he could see through the observation window everything was normal, with the earth, the now-distant moon, the sun and the stars. He could even see a tiny speck near the earth which he knew must be one of the man-made orbital stations. For all he knew it might be Station One, where Sir Eustace, Vale and Thor Eiriksson were waiting without having any idea that things were going desperately wrong.

"How much oxygen?" he asked quietly.

"Enough for eighty hours at least," said Scott. "Tanks are all right, I think. If we can't change course, we've just got to hope that Reggie and the others will cotton on, and come out to get us. They'll be able to track us by radar, and if they can't call us up they're bound to realize that we've got a problem."

Nigel hoped that he was right, but for the moment all they could do was to wait. Another two hours passed by—or, rather, crawled by; even though their oxygen tanks were still almost full, Nigel could not help looking regularly at the tell-tale red needle which would swing across to "empty" in less than four days. Running out of air was always the worst fear of the space-traveller, and there had been tragedies in the past both in space and on the unfriendly moon. Neither of the boys said much, and there was silence in the cabin except for Nigel's persistent but unsuccessful attempts to contact the Station.

Then, to his immense relief, he heard a faint sound in the earphones, above the ever-present hiss, and he tuned carefully. "Nigel Lorrimer to Base. Can you read me? Over!"

"Thor Eiriksson to ferry. What's the problem? Over!"

Clearly and calmly Nigel explained what had happened. "Just about the worst bang I can remember," he ended. "Motors still out of action, and we haven't a clue why. They look as though they ought to be all right, but they just don't work. Any ideas?"

"One or two, but I can't be sure." This time the voice was not Thor's; the brusque, forceful tone of Reginald Vale could not be mistaken. "Listen, both of you. If I'm correct—and I may not be—the trouble comes from one special point in space, and once you're out of the danger-zone you may be all right. Keep trying the motors. If they don't start up within the next hour I'll get another ferry and come out to you. Understood?"

"Understood. But—well, hang it all!" Scott turned on his transmitter. "We saw the same thing happening to the Station. What about your pet screen?"

"If it hadn't been for my screen we'd all be dead by now," snapped Vale. "As you know quite well if you take the trouble to think, we don't keep it switched on all the time, because there's no point, and it uses up more power than we can afford. It wasn't working when the first jolt came, and if I hadn't managed to get

22

across to the control room there's no knowing what the result would have been. It's working now, needless to say, and you two are very lucky that you weren't wiped out."

"Carl Brand—" began Nigel.

"I don't believe this has anything to do with Brand and his precious friends," said Vale shortly. "It doesn't look like Alpha to me, but in any case there's no point in yapping away until we've got you back inside the Station. An hour at most, and if you're still drifting, I'll see what I can do. Keep calling."

Nigel realized that the radio reception was getting steadily better; the loud hiss was sighing away to the soft crackle that was always there in the background, and he began to feel happier. Then a thought struck him. "Thor!"

"Yes?"

"What about Station Three? Didn't you say there had been a problem there too?"

"That's right. Gregory told me it was much the same as ours—sudden jolt, and loss of radio contact. Luckily they were able to get their screen working before anything else hit them, but I gather there's a lot more damage than there is here. We've sent out a general alarm, of course. Nobody down on earth seems to be any wiser than we are."

Another long pause, and Scott looked at his watch. Thirty minutes now, and still no sign that the power had come back. Once more he switched on; he hardly expected any response, but to his relief the rocket motors came to life, and within seconds were giving their familiar dull roar. "We're back," he said. "Get me a course, pal. Tell Reggie he needn't come for an early-morning flip after all!"

Thankfully Nigel called up, and made some quick calculations. The error in orbit was nothing like so great as he had feared, and he read out a string of figures; Scott used the motors skilfully, and both the boys relaxed. Evidently the rocket was unharmed, and it should be only a few minutes before they were back on their correct course. Then Vale came through again. "Hallo."

"Yes?"

"Keep your eyes skinned," said Vale. "We've been picking up some kind of message, but I can't make it out. It certainly doesn't come from earth; nobody in Control knows anything about it. The one base we can't contact is Station Eight. I'm going to take another ferry and go across there as soon as I can, but we've been out of touch with it for so long that I don't know its exact position, and I haven't been able to track it on the radar."

"Station Eight," repeated Scott slowly. "That's the new one. Aren't the Japanese running it?"

"That's right. Haro Noreiga's in charge; I don't know much about him except that he's a physicist, but I have come across Kaz Maramoto, who's up there too. It all seems rather hush-hush, and—oh, well, there's no point in guessing," said Vale. "Let me know as soon as you're ready to dock."

Another hour, and the earth was starting to look like a coloured map instead of a globe. Periodically Scott checked his orbit, and made alterations to the course he had set; communications were normal now, and to all outward appearances there was nothing wrong. Neither Scott nor Nigel felt in the least sleepy, though they had had nothing more than fitful dozes for many hours. "Orbit insertion," said Scott at last, and a short burst from the rocket motors gave a momentary feeling of pressure. "Fine. I reckon we'll be home in time for lunch."

"I wonder," muttered Nigel. "What did Reggie say about Station Eight?"

"Search me. We'll soon find out, I suppose."

In fact they had not long to wait. The warning light on the radio panel flashed, and Sir Eustace came through. "Hallo, young Nigel. Hallo, there. I take it you're safely in orbit?"

"We're coming in," said Nigel.

"Not so fast. Listen," said Sir Eustace. "Are you absolutely sure that your motors are functioning properly? Because if they're showing signs of missing on even one cylinder, you can forget what I was going to say."

"They're all right," said Scott. "We've plenty of oxygen, too. What's up?"

"That is precisely what I want to know. Let me explain the problem in words of one syllable." Sir Eustace paused. "As I've always said, I'm very old and doddery, but I do have hunches now and then. The last one turned out to be at least fifty per cent accurate, and since then I've come up with another. It's about Station Eight."

"What about it?"

"That's the point. As you may or may not have been told, Eight is a kind of experimental set-up. The Japs were responsible for it, and they still are. I've met Maramoto, who's a very pleasant chap, and there's also a rather nebulous gentleman named Noreiga, who appears to be one of the leading physicists of the Far East—at least, that's what Reggie says, and he ought to know. I can't believe there are more than four or five men on Station Eight all told, and I expect they're either Japanese or Chinese. They haven't told anyone much about what they're up to, and even International Science Control seems a bit vague."

"Do you think—"

"I don't really think anything, except that since all this trouble started Station Eight has gone silent. We've been calling up regularly, and we're not the only ones, but we can't get a squeak out of them. I'm just starting to wonder if they can be in worse condition than we were a few hours ago."

"And you want us to go and scout around?" asked Scott shrewdly.

"That was more or less what I had in mind," agreed Sir Eustace. "We've managed to get a radar bearing, and Eight shouldn't be hard to find. We could send out another ferry, and if you're in any doubt about your engines I'll do just that, but according to Thor's calculations you're almost within hailing distance. Do you feel like taking a look? If there's nothing the matter you can ask them to give you a cup of green tea, or whatever the Japanese drink, and then come straight home."

"We're game," said Nigel promptly. "We'll need a decent fix, though."

"Splendid. I thought you wouldn't mind," said Sir Eustace, still in that deceptively casual tone. "I'll pass you back to Thor, then. He's got all the details, and my feeble brain hasn't a hope of grasping all the mathematics. Keep in touch."

There was a pause, and then Thor came through, reeling off a stream of information which Nigel noted down. Scott gave a nod. "Looks straightforward enough. Here goes, then."

Navigating in space was much easier than it had been in the pioneer days, and "flying" from one orbital base to another was no problem at all; Scott had long since lost all count of the number of times that he had made these short-range trips. Yet as he adjusted the controls, and gave a first burst of power, he had a feeling of unease. Nigel felt the same, and as the rocket accelerated the boys exchanged a meaningful glance. "Not sure that I like it," said Scott. "Let's hope we don't find Carl Brand waiting for us. I've seen enough of him to last me a lifetime."

"Me too," muttered Nigel. "Want me to take over for a bit?"

"I'm O.K. You check on the radar, and let me know as soon as you pick up Eight."

For some time they flew on; in space there was no sensation either of motion or of weight except when the motors were working, and there was nothing to show that they were whirling round the earth at thousands of miles per hour. Below, they could see the outlines of Europe and Asia, partly covered with cloud; even England could be made out, looking very small and insignificant from so great a distance. Then they passed over the night side of the earth, and they could glimpse the lights of the great American cities. "Nothing yet," said Nigel at last. "We ought to be coming up before long, I reckon. Thor!"

"Yes?"

"Nothing from Eight? We haven't come within range yet."

"No messages," said Thor slowly. "Gregory says that the Russians have sent out a ferry too, but I don't know where it is. There must be something badly wrong."

"Unless it's a straight power failure," said Nigel. "I'll keep trying."

Another long interval, and then Nigel let out an exclamation. "There they are. At least, it's something . . . Come and look."

Scott swung across the cabin. The radar screen was not quite clear. In one corner there was a tiny "blip", and as they watched it grew in size. "It's Eight all right," muttered Scott. "It's—hang it all, it looks lopsided. Call up."

Nigel obeyed, but there was no answer, and the boys watched breathlessly as the blip on the screen swelled and swelled. There was no doubt now; it was Station Eight, but it was not intact. One of the long panels projecting from the main cylinder had been broken away, and the radio dish was floating freely; the whole Station was spinning round, and there was no sign of life. "It's—it's wrecked," breathed Scott. "Something must have crashed into it. If the air's rushed out—"

"We'll have to go in," said Nigel swiftly, and swung over to the controls. "I'll take it easy, though. Keep watching."

The Station was only a few miles away now, and it was painfully clear that it was a total wreck. Gaping holes showed in the cylinder, and as the ferry closed in there was still no sign of anyone aboard. "Reckon they're done for," muttered Scott. "Better get our suits on. We'll have to go right inside and see if there's anyone left."

Nigel began to reply, and then broke off. Something else was coming through; a faint, distorted voice that could only just be heard. Both boys strained their ears, and both gasped. "Did you get it?" whispered Nigel.

"I think so. Keep going."

The hiss in the receiver became louder, but then the voice was heard again, and this time there could be no mistake. "Keep away," Scott could make out. "Keep away. Do not come close. You are in danger!"

Chapter 3

THE BLACK HOLE

Scott seized the microphone, and spoke into it slowly and loudly. "Scott Saunders to Station Eight. Message received but not understood. Where are you? Over!"

The reply was prompt. "Noreiga to Saunders. We are inside Station Eight. Do not try to rescue us. Make all speed to leave the area. Over!"

"Saunders to Noreiga. Have you a rocket able to fly?"

"No. Our rockets are destroyed. Do not wait. You have little time!"

Scott looked quickly across at Nigel. "What do we do? I don't reckon we can leave them to it. I vote we go in."

"Nothing else for it," said Nigel, his face white. "I'll take her. You try to see what's up."

Again the motors roared briefly, and Station Eight grew in size until it filled the radar screen. "We are coming to take you off," said Scott steadily. "If you can reach your airlock, be ready to board our ferry. How many of you are there in the Station?"

"Two only: myself and Professor Maramoto. I tell you it is dangerous. You will be wise not to make the attempt!"

"We're coming in," rapped Scott, and struggled into his vacuum-suit; Nigel did the same, and worked skilfully to bring the ferry as close as possible to the crippled Station. Still there seemed no sign of danger, and to all appearances everything was normal, but Scott was under no delusions. "Are your suits safe?"

"Yes. We will come into the airlock."

Manœuvring a ferry was mainly a matter of practice, and in the ordinary way Nigel would have taken his time, but every moment he expected to feel another hammer-blow, and he risked coming up to the Station at a speed much greater than he would normally have done. Scott went through the lock, and the outer door swung back; fastening his safety-line, he swung out into space. Ahead of him was the ruined space-station, and he paused. Should he go inside, or wait? For a full minute he hung there, with the star-studded sky around and the brilliantly-coloured earth far in the distance; to one side the moon looked pale and shrunken. "All right?" came Nigel's voice.

"I can't see them—yes, there they are. They're coming out."

Two figures had appeared through the flapping door of the Station Eight airlock, moving unsteadily as the Station spun. Scott gestured. "Come across," he said calmly. "If there's trouble around, we'll have to get clear as soon as we can."

"We are grateful." The voice was clear, but with a strong accent; Scott recognized the unmistakable tone of a Japanese. "We will make haste."

Scott was already beside the airlock of the ferry, but

he could not help being intensely curious. "I don't get it. What's wrong?"

The two figures launched themselves across the gap, and clutched at Scott's safety line. "Look there, and you will see. We must not delay."

Scott turned, staring in the direction of the distant moon. He squinted through his transparent facepiece, and then gave a soft exclamation. Some way away—he could not tell exactly how far—he could see something unusual; it looked like a pale, shimmering light, but there was a distinct movement. "Looks like some kind of a whirlpool," he muttered. "Boy! it's new on me! What is it?"

"Something we have created," came the reply. "We have made a monster that may destroy us all. Hurry, please. If it comes close to us, we will die!"

Scott was not inclined to argue, and as the three crowded into the tiny airlock he pulled the outer door shut; air rushed into the compartment, and as soon as the indicator registered "normal" he drew back the inner door. Nigel dived over to the main panel. "All set?"

"Get going," said Scott briefly. "There's something odd out there, and I don't like the look of it—"

It was at that moment that the jolt came. It was not so violent as the first, but it was enough to throw Scott roughly against the wall, and once more he felt the unpleasant shuddering that they had met with earlier. Nigel did not wait. He brought the rocket motors into play, and the pressure built up as the ferry accelerated, not with its usual steady motion but with a strange, uneven series of jerks. Gradually the jolting subsided, and Scott pulled off his helmet; at least there was no serious damage, but it was only when the shuddering had stopped that he could clear his brain. Then he realized that both the rescued scientists were hanging limply away from the floor. "Give me a hand, pal. They've knocked themselves out cold."

He was right. It did not take long to strip off the helmets and vacuum-suits, and Scott recognized one of the men at once; he had met Maramoto several times, while the other Japanese was presumably Noreiga. Both were unconscious, and Noreiga had a dark bruise across his temple, but they were breathing easily, and Scott felt less alarmed. "Concussion, I expect. Not much we can do about it before we get back to Base. I'll call up." He tuned his transmitter. "Scott to Station One. Reading me?"

"We've been receiving you all the time," said Sir Eustace, "and I must say that you've been giving us some very nasty moments. Keep your motors running for the time being. We'll give you a course correction as soon as we can, but you'd better get well clear of that—well, that thing you saw. Believe me, it isn't friendly. If Reggie's right, it may cause us a great deal of bother."

"What is it?"

"Call it a force-field, and you won't be far wrong. All I ask is that you shouldn't go anywhere near it. Keep watching."

Scott bent down and made a quick examination of the two unconscious Japanese. Neither showed any sign

B

of coming round, and he gave a helpless shrug; he had a good working knowledge of first-aid, but so far as he could see there was nothing to be done except wait. Presently Thor came through. "Ready for a course check?"

"Right," said Nigel. "Go ahead." He took down Thor's instructions, and the ferry manœuvred until it was moving almost parallel to the earth's surface. "That's about it. How far?"

"You ought to sight us in less than half an hour. Keep calling, though. We'll have to switch off our electric screen when you're getting near."

The next minutes dragged by. Scott peered out of the narrow observation window; he could see a dot of light which could only be one of the other Stations, but he could also see a dim, misty glow which pulsated gently and sent out what seemed to be tongues of light. Then, to his relief, he caught sight of another speck which grew steadily until it showed up as the welcoming form of Station One, the base which he had come to regard as "home". "Coming in," he said. "For Pete's sake turn off the fence. We've had enough excitement for one day!"

"I've already switched it off, as you ought to have the sense to realize," said Vale. "We've been tracking you on the radar. Stop chattering, and get back as soon as you can."

It was comforting to come up to Station One, and to feel the usual slight bump as the ferry locked against the outer hull. The Station was not in the least like the sleek, wheel-shaped bases which had been planned almost a hundred years before, when flights to the moon still lay in the future; it was more like a cylinder with arms sticking out of it, and Sir Eustace had once commented that it looked like an orbital spider, but inside it was surprisingly roomy and comfortable, and it could hold a crew of at least thirty. One man—the Station commander, Richard Thomson—had been on board ever since the base had been built. He at least would never go back to earth; an accident had left him minus both his legs. On his home planet he would have been a cripple, but in the Station he was weightless, and being legless was no handicap at all.

Vale was the first to come through the airlock, looking as wildly untidy as usual. "Just as I thought," he said roughly, and stared at the unconscious men. "Are they badly hurt?"

"I don't think so. They'll come round all right, but they'll have sore heads for a bit," said Scott, and stretched himself wearily. "Boy, I feel all in . . . Is it Alpha?"

"I'm almost certain that it isn't. I'll explain later," snapped Vale. "You two have done enough for now, so you'd better go and clean yourselves up. We'll see to these beauties."

Scott realized that blood was standing out on his forehead; he had been so hard pressed that he had not noticed any pain, but by now his head was starting to throb, and he was only too glad to follow Nigel into the main body of the Station. The room that they shared in what was called Arm Two was very like an ordinary bedroom, except that it had no beds and was very small; because the space-men (and space-women!) spent so much of their lives in the Station, everything possible was done to make the living quarters comfortable. Of course there were differences, mainly because of the lack of weight; the old idea of spinning the Station round to produce artificial gravity had long since been given up as unnecessary. Scott washed the blood from his face, and yawned. "I'm done in. Wish I knew what that thing was!"

"What did Maramoto say? 'A monster that may destroy us all'," said Nigel thoughtfully. "It didn't look natural, anyway. It can't have been alive—"

Scott grinned. "Space-dragons and bug-eyed monsters?"

"Not likely. Robbie's one thing, but this is quite another. No, I guess it's some sort of experiment that's misfired."

"Can't be worse than Claude the Computer," muttered Scott; neither he nor Nigel would ever forget those terrifying moments when they had been under attack from a computer which had been built according to instructions picked up from an alien civilization many light-years away. "See here. What about using the telescope?"

Nigel looked thoughtful. "I don't know, but there's no harm in trying. I'll bet Peter and Juan are there."

The observatory of Station One lay at the end of the upper arm, as far away from the living quarters as possible. Not surprisingly, both Peter Monk and Juan Santos were in the dome, and Monk waved a hand in greeting. Both the astronomers were general favourites.

Monk, whose long face and beaky nose made him look rather like a parrot, had not been down to earth for at least three years, while his Spanish colleague made no secret of his dislike for being anywhere except on his beloved Station. "My dear Scott—Nigel. We're delighted to see you. Dear me, you've given us a great deal of worry!"

Scott grinned wryly. "That's nothing new. You know what we've been up to, then?"

"We have heard some things," said Santos in his broken English. "We were not happy. See! Our telescope, it is almost mended. We have made much working for it."

"No idea what caused the bump?"

"I think we're on the track," said Peter Monk cautiously, and handed Scott a piece of paper. "Examine that graph, please. You see the inked line?" Scott nodded. "Well, that is a measure of the X-rays we are picking up from one special point in space, and it is something quite out of the ordinary."

Nigel took the paper, and frowned. "X-rays?"

"Yes. As you know, X-rays are of very short wavelength, and most of them come either from the sun or from other star-systems millions of millions of miles away. This source is much closer. It is so unusual that I cannot be certain of anything, but—" Monk hesitated. "If it did not seem so absurd, I would say that these X-rays come from something even closer to us than the moon."

"I wonder," said Scott, and stared through the transparent section of the outer hull. "You know we saw a strange sort of glow, just before we were thumped by —by whatever it was? It looked close to Station Eight. At least, it was in the same part of the sky."

"Quite so. That is also where our X-rays are coming from," said Monk seriously. "Some time ago we tried to use the telescope. The repairs are not yet complete, and we had some difficulty, but we were able to make out a body which is most certainly not a star or a planet, or even part of a space-station. As soon as we have the instruments in full use again, we will attempt to find out just what it is."

"Can you see it now?"

"No, because it is on the other side of the earth, but it will return in less than one hour," said Santos, and looked at his watch; timekeeping on the Station was very different than on earth, but wrist-watches were still worn by almost all the astronauts. "I think we must now go to the control room, please. We have been asked to attend."

The control room was the nerve-centre of Station One. As well as the main radio and television equipment, it contained the panels from which the movements of the Station could be regulated; not that corrections were needed very often, but within limits the orbit could be changed by using the powerful rockets fitted to the outer hull. Equally important, perhaps, was the electronic screen that Vale had developed as a guard against Carl Brand and the Alpha organisation. Once the screen was switched on, no nuclear weapon could penetrate to within a mile of the Station, though whether it would be effective against this new and so far unknown enemy remained to be seen. Richard Thomson was waiting; with him were Thor Eiriksson, Sir Eustace, and the young Russian, Gregory Voronov, who spent most of his time on the Soviet-built Station Three, but who had become a close friend of Scott and Nigel. There was no sign of Vale, and Scott wondered whether he was still waiting to talk to the injured Japanese.

"Well done, both of you," said Thomson curtly. "You've had a lucky escape—not for the first time; I don't suppose it'll be the last, either," he added with a dry chuckle. "We're up against something new, and so far we're pretty much in the dark."

"Noreiga—" began Nigel.

"Noreiga and Maramoto aren't badly hurt, I'm glad to say. Reggie is with them now, and so is Constantine." Constantine Londos, the Greek doctor, had a medical reputation second to none, and it had been a relief when he had elected to stay on the Station rather than spend his time on earth. "We can't find out much more until they come round, but the first thing I want to do is to hear what you've got to tell us. It's important."

"You saw most of it." Nigel looked at Scott. "I was inside while the fun was going on."

Scott told his story; how they had sighted Station Eight, how they had see the strange glow, and what happened after Noreiga and Maramoto had been brought into the ferry. Thomson listened carefully, drumming his hand on the desk. "You've no real idea what it was, then? The glow, I mean?"

"Not a clue," said Scott. "All I can say that it was—well, it wasn't just staying still. It looked to me as if it was shooting stuff outwards, but it didn't seem exactly solid, either. I don't know what to make of it."

"And Maramoto said it was dangerous?"

"He did. He said that if it got too close, we'd be well and truly in the cart." Scott glanced across at Peter Monk. "Does that make sense?"

Monk looked thoughtful. "I have some ideas, but they sound so far-fetched that I think I'd prefer to keep them to myself until I have been able to talk to our Japanese friends," he said. "The thing is undoubtedly sending out X-rays, and I am quite sure that it isn't far away."

Thomson nodded. "All the Stations are doing their best to keep track of it, and so are the ground observatories, but everyone seems as puzzled as I am. Well, we'll have to wait for Noreiga and Maramoto. What about the other men on Station Eight?"

"There weren't any," said Gregory Voronov from the doorway. "We picked up a message a few hours ago, before the trouble started, and Dr. Noreiga told us that only the two of them were left on board. They must have been expecting something or other."

"If—" began Thomson, and broke off as Vale came in. "Any news, Reggie?"

"A good deal," said Vale harshly. "It's much worse than I'd expected. Those confounded idiots! I warned them they were tinkering with forces they didn't understand, but nothing would persuade them to listen to me. Sheer stupidity!"

"My dear Reggie! You sound somewhat annoyed," said Sir Eustace mildly. "Count ten, and start all over again. What exactly are you getting at?"

Vale glared. "I'm trying to tell you, if you'll have the goodness to let me get a word in edgeways. I've had to force it out of those two maniacs, and it was all I could do to stop myself from pitching them through the nearest airlock. Lunacy!"

"What particular type of lunacy?" asked Sir Eustace patiently. "You're not trying to tell me that they've produced a really good, old-fashioned bug-eyed monster or anything of that kind?"

"Worse." Vale paused, and drew a deep breath. "Listen, all of you. Noreiga and his precious team have been carrying out experiments with super-dense material. They were doing their best to go beyond all reasonable limits, and they've done it. What they've created is nothing more nor less than a black hole—and it's getting bigger all the time. Unless we can destroy it within the next few days, it may even swallow up the whole of the earth!"

Chapter 4

TRAPPED!

Scott let out a gasp, and stared at Vale blankly. "Swallow up the whole of the earth?" he repeated. "You're joking!"

"I was never more serious in my life," said Vale curtly. "To make matters even worse, if possible, I'm half afraid that Station One is well and truly in the danger-zone. Don't you understand?"

"I know I'm old and stupid," said Sir Eustace in his usual gentle tone, "but I'm bound to say that so far as I'm concerned the whole thing is as clear as mud. What exactly do you mean by a black hole? It sounds rather like something that goes bump in the night, but I don't gather how you can have a hole in space. Am I wildly off track?"

Vale gave an impatient gesture. "Do you want me to give you a lesson in elementary science?"

"I could certainly do with it," said Sir Eustace. "Frankly, my dear chap, I haven't the faintest idea of what you're talking about. Do explain in terms that even an ancient dimwit such as myself can understand."

Vale gave a sudden grin; he knew very well that Sir

Eustace's casual manner meant nothing at all. "All right, then. Do you know what a star is, and how it shines?"

"It goes twinkle, twinkle, twinkle; it's extremely hot, and I wouldn't want to go too close in. Is that what you mean?"

"Hardly. A star," said Vale, "is nothing but a huge nuclear reactor. Inside it, where the temperature is millions of degrees, one gas is changing into another, so that energy is set free. That's why the sun goes on shining, and why it won't change much for thousands of millions of years yet. When it uses up all its—well, its fuel, it will blow its outer layers away into space, the inside will shrink and become incredibly dense, and it'll end up as a very small, tightly-packed object called a white dwarf." He paused. "If you have a star which is more massive, it'll run wild, so to speak, and explode; that's what we call a supernova. And if you have a star which is more massive still, it will collapse as soon as it stops producing energy, and the collapse will be so sudden and so violent that nothing can stop it. Do you follow me so far?"

"More or less. At least, I think so."

Vale nodded. "Well, when our massive star becomes very small, the density is so high that a piece of it the size of a pin's head would weigh millions of tons. That means that the gravitational pull is so strong that not even light can escape from it—and light is the fastest thing in the universe. So the old collapsed star is surrounded by a sort of forbidden zone which is cut off from the rest of space. In fact, it's a black hole."

Sir Eustace looked puzzled. "You mean that Noreiga and Maramoto have produced a genuine, honest-to-goodness star?"

"Of course they haven't," said Vale impatiently. "What they were doing was to take a piece of ordinary material, and compress it so strongly that it would become the centre of a tiny black hole—a mini-hole, if you like. I won't try to explain just how they went about it, because I'm not sure myself, but the result was something they didn't expect, and that's what we're up against."

Peter Monk broke in. "This is disastrous," he said in a shaking voice. "If a black hole of any size is created, it cannot be destroyed. It will go on sucking in material from all around, and it will increase in size all the time—"

"Exactly. Now you're starting to see," said Vale grimly. "The thing's out there; it's a kind of space-cannibal, and it's eating up all the atoms within range of it. Within a few weeks it may have grown into something a thousand miles across. Once that happens, it'll be completely out of control."

There was a pause. "The X-rays," muttered Juan Santos. "I begin to see. If the black hole is dragging material inside it, there will be great heat caused, and this will mean that very powerful X-rays are sent out. This is terrible!"

Sir Eustace straightened up. "Quite so," he said calmly. "What you're saying is that if nothing can be done, this monster will go on swallowing more and more material until there'll be nothing left of the earth, or you, or me. Over to you, Reggie. We're in your hands."

Vale shrugged. "I won't try to fool you. I haven't the slightest idea of how we can tackle it. This is a situation I've never come across—I needn't tell you that!—and I'm not even clear why the experiment went so wrong so quickly, but when Maramoto gave me an inkling of what he was trying I did warn him not to push his luck too far. Unfortunately, he didn't pay any attention. Peter, when does it come back into view from here?"

"In a few minutes, if it has kept to the same path round the earth," said Monk, and rubbed his nose thoughtfully. "If you have no objection, we will return to the observatory. I will do my best to find out how this thing is developing."

"Splendid. Let's hope it's fizzling out," said Sir Eustace cheerfully. "One never knows, I suppose. Personally, I'm going to start sending a few urgent messages down to earth. Reggie, I suggest that you see what you can get out of our Japanese friends. They know more about it than anyone else."

Vale snorted. "I'll do my best, but I can't promise much, and I haven't even any proper ideas yet; we're working blind. I'm absolutely baffled by that jolt we felt. I can only think that it was some kind of a shock-wave, but how can you have a shock-wave in empty space? It makes no sense at all."

"It was like being bashed by a hammer," muttered Scott. "I thought we were done for, and no mistake."

"You nearly were. I simply don't know what to make

of it," said Vale savagely. "Get back to the observatory, and keep watch. All we can do at present is to send out a general alert, and make sure that our electronic screens are working at full blast, though I've no idea whether they'll be able to give us proper protection."

The observatory in Arm Four had been designed to give as clear a view of surrounding space as was possible. Scott did not pretend to understand the various complicated instruments and recorders scattered around, and the main telescope was still partly out of action. Santos looked angry. "This is bad," he said. "We must hasten with our workings. Please to watch."

"Where's the thing likely to be?"

"You should see it—there," said Santos, and pointed. "I think it will be more bright than when it was last visible."

Scott and Nigel waited. For some time nothing unusual could be seen; the earth, the moon and the stars were their usual familiar selves, and there seemed little to say. Presently the inner door opened, and Monk looked round. "My dear Maramoto. You have recovered, I trust?"

"Thank you yes. I am sorry to have been the cause of this trouble." The Japanese scientist looked tired and ill, but his voice was steady. "It has been a lesson to me, I admit. We should have taken much more notice of what Dr. Vale was saying."

"Look here, though," said Nigel. "It's—well, I don't follow even now. How did you make this black hole thing, and why?"

46

Maramoto sighed. "It was a purely scientific experiment, you understand. I am a physicist, and so is Dr. Noreiga. If we could study highly-compressed material from close range, we could learn much from it, and so we tried a new method which we had developed. For a time all went well, but somehow we were not happy. That is why we alone stayed on Station Eight."

"It was all pretty hush-hush," said Scott suspiciously.

Maramoto gave a slight shrug. "We wished to work undisturbed, and we had no thought that we could put others in danger. When we connected up our main transmitters, there was a reaction that took us by surprise. The material we were trying to condense was carried in a small capsule some distance from the Station, and we could not tell that the result would be so violent. We thank you for coming to our rescue."

"Not much else we could do," said Scott. "What caused that jolt, though?"

"I cannot tell. One cannot have a shock-wave in space, because there is nothing to carry it, so it must have been an effect of an unknown nature. We can do little now before we find out whether or not the black hole is spreading. Dr. Vale has asked me to tell you that he needs a photograph as soon as possible."

"We will do our best, but it will not be easy," said Monk, and stared out into the star-studded blackness. "It will appear at any moment . . . Ah. Look there. I am not mistaken, surely?"

"It's a glow all right, and it isn't a star," said Nigel, straining his eyes. "It's moving, too, but I can't see any shape to it. Must be the hole!"

All five concentrated upon the dim, ghostly light in the far distance. It was larger than they had expected, and they could make out a slight flickering; Santos swung the telescope, and then gave an exclamation of annoyance. "The drive is still not in order. We must wait."

Minutes passed. For a while the glow brightened, but then it faded again, and Monk gave a helpless shrug. "It has changed its path, and for the moment it will come nowhere near us. Dear me, this is most unfortunate. I have half a mind to take a ferry and see whether I can obtain a better view——"

"Not on your life," said Scott firmly. "You'd aim yourself in the wrong direction, and end up near the Pole Star!" Monk gave a sad smile; he was well aware of his lack of skill as a pilot, and Scott grinned back. "See here, though. Do you really mean that Reggie wants a close-up picture?"

"It would help," said Maramoto. "Yes, it would help, but we can only trust that one of the other Stations will be better placed——"

"Why wait? We can take a rocket and go for a ride," said Scott, and Nigel nodded. "Can't do any harm, and it's a lot better than sitting about doing nothing. What about it?"

"Ask Reggie," said Nigel. "I'm all for it."

Both Vale and Thomson were in the control room, and rather to Scott's surprise neither made any objection. "It might be valuable," said Thomson thoughtfully. "What do you say, Reggie?"

"Provided that you keep your heads, it shouldn't be

particularly dangerous," said Vale. "You won't have to go really close in, and I'd very much like a spectrum. In case you've forgotten what a spectrum is, it's a picture taken with an instrument which can split up light and find out what's causing it." Scott gave a chuckle. "You're sure?"

"Of course we're sure. What about an orbit, though?"

"I've been working on that for the past hour, so I can get you a course to set. It'll take me some time to get my bits and pieces fixed up, and I'll need Thor as well; he's getting to the stage when he knows almost as much about scientific instruments as I do, which is saying something. Go and check out one of the ferries."

"You—"

"Of course I'm coming," snapped Vale. "Oh, I won't leave you two behind; I'm bound to admit that both of you can pilot a rocket better than I can, but have the goodness to do exactly as you're told. Get busy."

Scott and Nigel did not argue. Once Vale had made up his mind nothing would change it, and there was no sense in trying. Station One carried half a dozen ferry rockets, most of which could hold four people comfortably, and Sir Eustace had made a firm rule that they should be kept in readiness for any emergency— a policy which had been proved wise time and time again. Thor joined them, and helped in making a thorough inspection of the equipment and propulsion units. "Quite like old times," he said lightly. "Remember when you came to hook us off that weird asteroid?"

"I'm not likely to forget it," grunted Nigel. "Say,

where's Gregory? He was in that spot of bother too, remember."

"Gregory's gone back to Station Three. The Russians have been trying to get a sight of Basil, but I don't know whether they've had any luck."

"Who the blazes is Basil?"

Thor broke into a laugh. "Basil the Black Hole. I needn't tell you that that's what Sir Eustace has started to call it, and I can't get it out of my head. Reggie doesn't see the funny side of it, though."

It was some time before Vale came through the airlock, carrying a clumsy-looking instrument that bore a faint resemblance to a telescope. "All set," he said curtly. "I've got a really reliable orbit, thanks to the Russians, and the range won't be more than a few hundred miles. We'll blast off in ten minutes."

"Where's Basil now?"

"If you mean the black hole, it's moving in a path which takes it out to almost a thousand miles above ground level. Stop chattering, and get ready. Remember to do exactly what you're told, because if we get too close we may be in for a jolt strong enough to smash us to bits. Nigel, you handle the communications; Thor, your job is to get a decent spectrum. Strap down."

Scott settled himself at the controls, and made a final check of the instrument panel. Then Nigel called up on the radio. "Ferry to Station One. Permission to blast off, please."

Sir Eustace replied. "On your way, my lucky lads. Have a nice trip, and give Basil my regards when you see him. Don't forget to call up every few minutes. According to our friend Maramoto, you might be in for all sorts of excitement if you're not careful. He even said something about ending up in a completely different universe, which isn't my idea of a happy outing. Good luck!"

Vale handed Scott a pad covered with figures. "There's the orbit. Keep to it, whatever happens, and don't let your attention wander even for a second, because we may be in for a rough ride."

Scott studied the figures, and switched on. The rocket motors started up, and there was a soft jerk as the ferry undocked; then they were clear of Station One, and moving gently away. Before long the great base had faded into the distance. Far away they could see two more of the Stations, but for the moment there was no sign of Basil.

Nigel made regular calls to Station One, and then tuned in to Station Three, which was officially controlled by the Russians. At once he recognized the voice of Boris Tansky, the Moscow astronomer. "We have not made the calculations of a good orbit, because this—what is it?—this hole seems to be moving around," said Tansky. "It is very strange, you understand. It has moved some way from what is left of the eighth station. What are your plans, please?"

"We're going to try for a close-up picture," said Nigel. "Tell me one thing, though. Is the black hole going near any of the other bases?"

"We do not know," said Tansky. "There is a warning that Base Five may be threatened, but we are uncertain. Please, is Dr. Vale with you?"

"Yes. He and Thor are going to try for the photographs."

Tansky clicked his tongue. "It is necessary to take great care, you understand. Not only is this hole active, but it is growing in size. We in our Soviet station are ready to be of help."

"Thanks a lot," said Nigel. "We'll call you if we get into big trouble. Out."

It was at least two hours more before they had their first sight of the mysterious glow, and even then it was so dim that Scott could not be sure of it. Vale joined him at the observation window, and muttered impatiently. "Confound it all, I'm getting as blind as a bat. We'll have to get a lot closer than this if I'm to get any results that are worth having, and I'll have to switch on the screen; I daren't leave it any longer."

"Why not?" asked Nigel.

"Because I haven't the slightest wish to be bombarded by dangerous X-rays, you idiot," snapped Vale. "You've already been told that Basil—confound that ridiculous name!—is sending out X-radiation in large quantities, and unless we protect ourselves there are bound to be some very nasty after-effects. Thank goodness the screen will shield us from that sort of thing, anyway. Scott!"

"Yes?"

"Any idea of the range?"

"Hard to tell. About four hundred miles, I guess," said Scott slowly, "but I can't get a radar reading. If

Basil wasn't glowing, there wouldn't be any way of telling that he's there."

"Quite so. That's part of the danger; radar isn't the slightest use," said Vale. "Close the range, but sheer off at the slightest sign of trouble with the motors. I don't think the main zone spreads out far from the hole itself, but I may be wrong. Report back, Nigel."

Nigel turned, and raised his earphones. "That's just what I was doing. There's something brewing, I believe, and Base said they'll come through again in a few moments. Listen out."

There was a pause, and then Thomson spoke. "Base to ferry. Listen carefully, please. We've just heard that an attempt is to be made to destroy the black hole, and it may be wise for you to leave the area. The attempt will take place in less than an hour from now."

"What the blazes are you trying to do?" barked Vale.

"We're not trying to do anything ourselves, my dear fellow," said Sir Eustace soothingly. "This wasn't our idea at all, but the boys down on earth are getting worried. In fact, it's not too much to say that Basil is scaring the pants off them, and all sorts of wild and woolly ideas have been floating around. The scheme is to take a pot-shot at Basil with one of the best nuclear squibs that the United Nations can lay their hands on. I'm quite sure it won't upset Basil one little bit, but I suppose there's no reason why they shouldn't have a try."

"Nuclear bomb? Ridiculous." Vale gave a snort. "That'll be about as much good as using a pea-shooter, even if they manage to aim it in the right direction—and from what I know of the United Nations, they'll be bound to bungle the whole thing. We'll wait around. I haven't got the photographs yet, and I don't mean to go back empty-handed."

"Up to you, but watch your step," said Sir Eustace. "I'll let you know as soon as the banger is well and truly on its way."

Vale swung back across the cabin, and settled himself beside Scott in the control position. "We'll go in as close as we dare. I don't think there's any real risk so long as we stay beyond a hundred miles or so, but I can't be certain, so check your motors all the time. Understand?" Scott nodded. "All right, then. Get busy."

Scott gave a brief burst of power, and the ferry accelerated, moving outward from earth and toward the orbit of the glow. Gradually the light increased, and Scott could make out the flashing, unsteady movements that he had seen before; they were much more pronounced now. "Range two hundred. Enough?"

"Not yet. I've got some useful pictures, but they're still blurred," said Vale. "At least, I'm fairly sure they are. Change the exposure, Thor. It looks to me as if we're dealing with a temperature of hundreds of thousands of degrees—"

"Why aren't we melting, then?" muttered Nigel.

Vale glared. "Because a high temperature doesn't necessarily mean a great deal of heat. Confound it all, that's elementary science. High temperature means that the bits of material are whirling around at tremendous speeds, and in this case, thank goodness, there aren't enough of them to burn us up. Take us in closer, Scott."

Scott obeyed. The glow was brightening all the time, and it filled the cabin with an unearthly radiance that seemed to be full of menace. "X-ray counter out of action," said Thor. "There's too much radiation for it to cope. I've never seen anything like it."

"Neither have I," said Vale, and looked across at Nigel. "For your information, we're bathed in a flood of X-rays that would kill us within five minutes but for the protective screen round us. Look at it!" He gestured. "Material is being sucked into the black hole, and before it goes inside it's whirled around so fast that the temperature shoots up to an incredible value. Deadly dangerous, but fascinating as well—"

"Look there," broke in Scott abruptly, and pointed. "What's that?"

Another moving speck of light had appeared. It was still a long way off, but it was shifting rapidly against the background of stars, and it became brighter every moment. "Must be the bomb," muttered Thor. "What do you reckon will happen, Reggie?"

Vale gave a mirthless grin. "Remember what I said about using a pea-shooter? Well, we'll soon see. At least they seem to have aimed it correctly, which is more than I'd have expected from those nitwits down at United Nations headquarters. I think we're out of the danger-zone, so I suppose we may learn something. I'll get as many photographs as I can."

Scott cut the motors, and there was silence as the

ferry drifted along in free fall. "It's going to miss," breathed Nigel. "It's veering away to the right—"

"It won't miss," said Vale. "Within a few dozen miles, the gravitational pull of the black hole will suck it in. Remember, there's a piece of incredibly dense material in the middle of the hole, and it's got tremendous power, even though I don't suppose it's any larger than a pin's head. Watch, and you'll see what I mean."

All four crowded round the observation window, and kept their eyes on the moving speck. With deceptive slowness it moved toward the flashing glow, and then, suddenly, it accelerated; it seemed to rush toward the centre of the luminous patch, and Scott held his breath. What would happen? Then he let out a gasp. There was a burst of light, and the moving speck exploded. For an instant it shone almost as brilliantly as the sun, and then it was gone. "You see?" said Vale. "Just as I expected. As soon as it came within the danger-zone, it was wiped out. That's what would happen to us if we were crazy enough to get too near."

"Pretty grim," muttered Scott. "Basil doesn't seem exactly friendly, does he? I reckon we'd better get clear while the going's good."

Vale shrugged. "We're all right where we are, and in any case that bomb went off because the nuclear reactor was triggered; that was the main problem, as the United Nations people should have realized. I don't think I can do much more. All right, then; we'll go back."

"I've got a course," said Nigel. "Here you are, pal."

Scott nodded, and made a quick calculation. Then

he set the readings on the main panel, and depressed the lever which should have brought the rocket motors into play. To his alarm, nothing happened; there was no sound, and he felt a surge of panic. Vale looked over. "What's the matter? Trouble with the motor?"

"It won't fire," said Scott thickly. "It's dead. It must be that thing out there. We're trapped!"

Chapter 5

A BRUSH WITH DEATH

Vale muttered under his breath, and looked savagely at the control panel. "This is my fault," he said bitterly. "I ought to have had more sense. Keep trying, Scott."

Scott obeyed, but with no result; the motors stayed silent, and to all intents and purposes the ferry had turned into a helpless, drifting hulk. "No go. I can't do a thing."

"What's the range?" asked Thor steadily.

"Well over a hundred. Should have been far enough, but—well, it may have been some effect due to that infernal bomb," snapped Vale. "What worries me most is that if our protective screen fails we'll be in the thick of the X-rays, which wouldn't be at all nice. You'd better call up Base, I suppose. We'll have to let them know where we are."

"I can't get through," said Nigel. "All I can get is a crackle loud enough to drown anything they're saying. I haven't a clue whether they can hear me, either. I don't expect they can."

"So we're out of touch as well as out of power. I wish I knew what to do, but I'm bound to admit that this has taken me by surprise." Vale removed his bat-

58

tered spectacles, and polished them vigorously. "What about the fuel, Scott? If we've plenty of reserve there is one thing I might try, but it's risky."

"Tanks almost full. We didn't use much fuel coming over here," said Scott; he was badly frightened, but nothing would have made him show it. "If we could give even one burst, we might get clear. What are you getting at?"

"I'm not sure myself. Let me think," said Vale curtly, and turned back toward the window; for some minutes he said nothing, and there was utter silence in the cabin. Then Thor spoke. "Range decreasing," he said quietly. "Looks as though we're being sucked into the black hole. This could be 'it'—"

"I don't think so," said Vale. "Listen to me, all of you. There's one chance left, and it's up to you to decide whether we take it or not. I warn you that it'll be as dangerous as anything we've ever faced, but if we don't try it we are bound to end by being pulled inside that infernal thing, which would be fatal. The whole ferry would be torn to pieces. We haven't long to make up our minds—"

"What do you mean to do?" asked Scott, his face white.

"Switch off our screen," said Vale bluntly. "I may be making the blunder of a lifetime, but I've a feeling that if we had only a few per cent more power we could break free. Using the protective screen means that we're taking a lot of energy from the main circuits, and adding that to the ordinary rocket motor might do the trick. I can't guarantee it, but it seems possible."

"But—" Scott looked helpless. "Didn't you say that without the screen we'd be slap bang in the X-radiation?"

"I did, and I was right. I told you it was risky," said Vale. "If we turn off the screen for a few seconds we'll survive, but even a minute might be too long. X-rays are unpleasant things, especially when they're being sent out in large quantities. Well, what about it?"

"Not much choice, is there?" said Scott, hoping that he sounded more confident than he felt. "If it's either X-rays or Basil, give me the X-rays every time."

Vale looked across at Nigel and Thor; both nodded. "All right, then. It'll take me a minute or two to make sure I can flip the screen back on without any hold-up, but I'll be as quick as I can. I'll need your help, Thor."

Rapidly he eased himself across to the rear compartment of the ferry; Thor followed, and Nigel went on with his fruitless efforts to contact Sir Eustace. "Not a peep," he said gloomily. "Crackle's getting louder, too. I wonder if they've any idea that we're in the cart?"

"They must know something's up. We've been out of touch for well over an hour, and we were told to call out every few minutes," said Scott. "Boy! look there. We're being sucked in. Range a hundred and fifty now, and decreasing. I can't take a lot more!"

The glow was brightening every instant, and for the first time both boys could see the darting tongues of luminosity that came from the blurred edge of the patch. "Like a firework show," breathed Nigel. "Gee! Who'd have thought we'd see anything like that? If—"

He broke off. The ferry had shuddered slightly but noticeably, and Scott clamped his arms round the control lever. "Basil's getting ready for us," he said as lightly as he could. "Reckon we'll be due for a bumping any time now. Can you see anything?"

"Don't look straight at it," barked Vale, plunging back into the cabin. "Yes, I know the windows protect our eyes from X-rays and almost everything else, but this is something new. Range?"

"Down to a hundred and ten. Getting less."

Again came an ominous jolt, and Vale clenched his hands. "Strap down. If we don't chance it now, we'll be too late. Want me to take over, Scott?"

"I'm all right," said Scott steadily. "Full power when you say the word?"

"Yes. Give it everything you've got, and keep at full thrust. I don't know whether the motor will fire or not, but at least there's a chance." Vale gave a quick glance through the observation window. "One extra danger is that the way we're pointing, we may blast toward the hole instead of away from it, but that can't be helped. Get ready. I'll count three, and then switch the screen off."

Scott set his lips; he was as scared as he had ever been in his life, but he managed to take a grip on himself. "Steady, boy," he muttered under his breath, and tensed as he hard Vale starting to count. One . . . two . . . three . . . and Scott switched on. The effect was immediate. The rocket motors started up, not with their usual roar but with a faltering scream; there was a thud, and the ferry pitched wildly. "Keep going," roared Vale. "I daren't give it much longer—"

Pitch-jerk! Then, for an instant the motors picked up, and Scott felt himself being pressed back against his couch. "Full power," he gasped. "Range steady— no, we're still closing in!"

"That's what I'd expected," rapped Vale, "but with any luck we've enough extra velocity to swing us round without being sucked in. Let me know if the motors cut again—if they do, I'll have to risk turning off the screen for another few seconds, but I don't want to."

"It's turned on now, then?"

"Of course it is. The extra power seems to have done the trick. Keep full thrust going!"

Scott raised himself up in his straps; he had a clear view through the front observation window, and what he saw made him let out a cry of amazement. Ahead, the glow was blinding, and it had taken on a bluish colour; the flashing had become more vivid, and Scott could see something else—a kind of spiralling movement all round the edge of the glow. He could not bring himself to take his eyes away from the window, even though the brilliance had become painful. Then he gulped as he felt the motors falter. "Now for it," he thought, but after a second or so the roar became steady again, and he heard Nigel's voice. "Boy, oh boy! Look!"

For an instant Scott thought he could see a break in the flashing ring of light; beyond, there was nothing— the stars were blotted out, and it was as though he were looking into a bottomless pit. Then they were past, and once more the ferry lurched as another shock-wave struck it. "We're through," panted Vale. "That was touch and go. Any damage?"

"None that I can see," said Nigel hoarsely. "How about you, Thor?"

The Icelander turned his head, and gave a wry smile. "I was busy taking photographs," he said simply. "If it's any help, I believe I've got the first-ever close-range views of the outside of a black hole, but it's not something I'd care to do again!"

Vale broke into a laugh. "Good for you, young Thor. Yes, we're well clear now; you can relax for the time being. I don't believe you know how lucky we've been. Motors steady, Scott?"

Scott nodded.

"Good," said Vale in a tone of deep satisfaction. "I didn't cut the screen for more than a second, and that wasn't long enough for the X-rays to do us any real harm. It's taught me a lesson, though," he added. "That whole thing can't be more than the size of a truck, but its pull is enormous. If we hadn't picked up enough speed, we'd have been sucked straight in."

"Size of a truck?" echoed Scott. "Must be bigger than that, surely."

"I doubt it. As I've told you, the piece of condensed material causing the black hole—that's to say, the material that Noreiga and Maramoto made—can't be more than half an inch across at most, and it's probably much less. What we're seeing is what we call the 'event horizon'—the edge of the black hole itself. Once inside that, you wouldn't get out again even if you could avoid being torn to pieces," said Vale. "Well, we've learned something at least. Radio still useless?"

"The crackling's getting less," said Nigel.

It was not long before the background hiss had died away to normal, and then Sir Eustace's voice came through. "Well, well, well. You seem to have been having a fascinating time," he said. "I gather you decided to pay Basil a social call?"

"Not quite," said Nigel grimly. "It was pretty scary."

"So I can tell. We've got some news for you, too," said Sir Eustace, "but I don't particularly want to broadcast it, because plenty of people will be listening in, and there's panic enough all round. I suggest you get home as soon as you can. I promise I'll have afternoon tea and buns waiting for you."

In fact the journey back to Station One was uneventful; the deadly glow faded into a speck, and to all outward appearances everything was normal, but Thomson soon made the real situation clear. "Earth's getting into a panic state," he said, looking round the control room; Sir Eustace was nowhere to be seen, but Vale was there, and so were Noreiga and Maramoto, both looking pale and anxious. "There's been a special meeting of the United Nations, and some pretty hard things are being said about us."

"About Japan, I fear," said Noreiga quietly. "We must accept all blame. It was a serious mistake."

"No good going back over all that," snapped Vale. "I warned you that you were playing with forces you didn't understand, but I can't really blame you. It was sheer bad luck that the experiment got out of control."

Noreiga gave a slight shrug. "You are kind, my friend, but we feel deeply responsible. We will do all we can to make amends."

"At the moment," said Thomson, "I'm not sure that we can do anything at all. It depends on whether this infernal thing is going to go on spreading. I'm told there's a chance that it may simply vanish."

"Fizzle out, you mean?" muttered Scott. "Gee! It didn't look much like fizzling out to me. I've never seen anything so scary."

"We'll soon know, because it must be fast approaching its critical size." Vale polished his spectacles. "Once it passes that stage, it'll swell out quickly unless we can prevent it, and that won't be easy—to put it mildly. I've got a call booked through to Kitt Peak. If anyone can get a fix on the thing, it'll be Alan Underhill."

Scott knew Professor Underhill, the director of America's greatest observatory. He had been to Kitt Peak, in Arizona, more than once, and had even been allowed to use the 300-inch reflecting telescope, by far the largest in the world. "How do you know the thing's in view from there?"

"Because I've worked it out," said Vale. "Make yourself useful, please, and get through to the Peak. There's all manner of interference, I know, but you should be able to call them."

Thor went to the television set, and switched on. For some moments nothing could be seen except sparks and flashes, but then the screen cleared, and a face came into focus. "Kitt Peak to Station One. Who are you calling, please?"

c

Vale thrust forward. "Vale to Underhill. It's urgent."

"Thank you. Please remain tuned in. Professor Underhill was expecting to hear from you."

"I'm not surprised," said Vale, and turned as Sir Eustace came in. "Anything new? At the moment we're all fiddling about wondering what to do, and it's quite infuriating."

"Well," said Sir Eustace cautiously, "it's really getting quite dramatic, and the johnnies at the United Nations are screaming blue murder. One of them—I forget who—even said that all space-men were dangerous maniacs who ought to be locked up in the nearest looney-bin, which strikes me as being a little extreme. I've done my best to calm things down, but I admit that I haven't been brilliantly successful. Ah! Alan Underhill, unless my aged eyes deceive me."

Professor Underhill looked surprisingly young to be in charge of the world's greatest observatory; he might have appeared even more youthful but for his neat black beard and trim moustache. "It's a bad business," he said slowly. "I take it you've heard about the communications blackout?"

"What?"

"All over the States," said Underhill. "It lasted for the best part of an hour, and that was the time that the black hole was above our horizon. There were all sorts of power failures, too. Hospitals were hit—"

Maramoto gave an exclamation. "This is terrible!"

"You haven't heard the worst yet," said Underhill. "Last time the thing passed over, which wasn't long

66

ago, we got a whole heap of information. It's just coming up to the critical size now. Next time we see it, we'll be able to tell whether it's going to go on growing or not. My guess is that it will—and once that happens, there'll be no way of stopping it!"

Chapter 6

A DESPERATE PLAN

There was a long pause. "I think I see what you mean," said Sir Eustace at last. "As you know, my ignorance of science is complete, but let me put it in my own simple way." He cleared his throat. "Point One: our Japanese friends have been trying to make ultra-dense material, and they've succeeded only too well. Point Two: they've made an object so dense that it's pulling in other material from all round it. Point Three: as soon as anything gets inside the boundary, or event horizon, it can't get out again—not even light. Point Four: if it goes on gobbling up everything in sight, it may end by gobbling up not only us, but the earth as well, complete with Aunt Mary and the kitchen sink. Am I on the right track?"

"Don't waste time," said Vale shortly, and turned back to the figure in the screen. "From what I can work out, the thing is due to come over your horizon again in about a quarter of an hour, so there may be another blackout. I'd like all the information you can give me. How about the side effects?"

"Power failures; electrical disturbances, and more to

come. I've been getting reports of storms and hurricanes all over Australia, and there's a whole lot of damage," said Underhill soberly. "I don't know how big the hole's got by now, but the power is enough to gum up the works well and truly. Better watch out. You're not in the same orbit, but you may be too close for comfort."

"If—" began Vale, and broke off as the screen went suddenly blank. Thor tuned carefully, but with no result, and Vale muttered angrily. "Keep trying. I've half a mind to go out myself and see how the hole's developing, but I just haven't enough time. So far as I can see, there's only one answer."

"What?"

"I'll tell you as soon as I've straightened it out in my mind," said Vale impatiently. "It may be a wild scheme, anyway, because we still don't know what we're really up against."

"Not quite, my friend," said Maramoto quietly; Scott had almost forgotten the two Japanese scientists. "We have had some experience, as you know. Permit us to offer any assistance in our power."

"I'll need it. In fact I wouldn't have any sort of a chance without you," said Vale dryly. "I've got some questions to ask, and then we'll put our heads together and see whether I'm crazy or not. Scott!"

"Yes?"

"Do you feel equal to taking a probe and having another look? Not too close, or you'll be caught in the same way as we were last time, but if you stay out beyond six or seven hundred miles you'll be safe enough, and I need to know how the size has changed over the last few hours."

"Checking up on Basil? I'm not sure that I approve," murmured Sir Eustace. "What do you say, Richard?"

"Up to them," said Thomson briefly. "I wouldn't try to stop them."

"We'll have a go," said Scott. "We'll know more about it this time, at least."

Vale turned toward the door. "Good. You'll find us in the laboratory. Report by radio as long as you can, and then come straight back to the Station. You'd better go too, Thor; if there's any trouble with the electric screen, you can handle it better than anyone else."

Scott was too tensed-up to feel tired. Nigel was in the same state, and followed automatically as Scott and Thor made their way to the docking port. "How close do you reckon we can get? We've had one dose of friend Basil, and I don't want another."

"No need to get too near," said Thor quietly; for once his Icelandic accent was noticeable—a sure sign that his nerves were on edge. "Check out, while I calculate an orbit."

Both Scott and Nigel were much too experienced to be careless over the flight-check of the ferry. Accidents were generally due to human error, as they knew, and there was no sense in running unnecessary risks. It was forty minutes before they were satisfied, and then Scott strapped himself down; they blasted gently away, and the ferry drifted out from Station One. "I can't raise any of the earth stations," said Nigel. "Too much interference. I reckon we'll lose contact altogether in a few minutes."

Scott shrugged. "Can't be helped. So long as the motors don't play any tricks we ought to be safe enough, I suppose. Here we go."

Station One shrank into a bright point of light. They were over the night hemisphere of the earth, and the glows of cities were visible below, but suddenly Nigel noticed something else, and pointed through the observation window. "See there."

"What?"

"Looks like a darned great fire," breathed Nigel, and strained his eyes. "Boy, it's big. Where the heck are we?"

"Over Australia," said Thor. "You're right. Underhill said there'd been trouble there, and that's more than an ordinary bush fire. Can't you get through to any of the earth stations?"

Nigel shook his head. "I've told you there's too much hiss. Nothing I can do about it."

Below them the menacing glow was unmistakable, but as the ferry flew on it faded, and before long there was nothing but blackness. Then, gradually, they came over the day-side of the earth, but they were too high up to make out much detail. Instead Scott and Thor strained their eyes for the first sign of the glow marking the position of the black hole, while Nigel continued his futile battles with the radio.

Once the rocket motors faltered, and Scott let out a

cry, but they picked up again at once, and he turned to Thor. "I don't think that was anything much. How far now?"

"We should be within range in three to four minutes. Direction 225 degrees—that puts it over there," said Thor, and gestured toward the observation window. "Keep your eyes skinned."

They were back over the night-side of the earth now, and the stars shone down with their usual steely brilliance; the moon was out of view, but Scott could see a red speck which he knew to be the planet Mars—without doubt Man's next target in space; already there were plans for sending an expedition to it. Then Scott gave an exclamation. "There's Basil. It must be!"

"Right," said Thor swiftly. "Range seven hundred miles. Get ready to blast away the second I tell you."

"What are you going to do?"

"Photograph it. I can work out the size from that," said Thor, and forced his body close to the window. "I don't like the look of it."

Nigel drew in his breath sharply. "It's growing, then?"

"I think so. Wait." Thor operated the camera, and then looked at Scott. "Can you chance going in a bit closer?"

"We'll try," said Scott, and made a course correction. Now he could see the glow more clearly, he realized that it had changed its whole appearance. There was a soft outline of radiance, but there was also a strange blackness—not the usual blackness of space, but a wide area where no stars could be seen. "Talk

72

about a hole," he muttered. "That's just what it is. It seems to have swallowed up the stars!"

"It's blocking their light, that's all," said Thor, and made another series of exposures. "That's about as near as I want to get. Better move away."

It was then that a soft jolt came, and Scott wasted no time. He gave the motors full power, and the pressure built up until all three were gasping for breath; it was not often that the rockets in a ferry were used at maximum thrust, and Nigel gave a gulp. "Steady on, pal. Easy does it."

"I'm not hanging about," said Scott grimly. "One visit to Basil is more than enough. I'm getting out while the going's good."

To his immense relief the motors showed no sign of faltering, and slowly the uncanny object faded from view, but then Scott had another thought. "What about our course? I've a pretty good idea of our orbit, but a decent fix would help if you can call anyone over the radio."

"I'm doing my best," said Nigel slowly, "but there's something all wrong, quite apart from this darned hiss. I can get a message of some kind, but it isn't on the right wavelength . . . yes, there it is again. This is crazy!"

"How come?"

"That was one of the Stations, but—well, it's in the wrong part of the radio band," said Nigel helplessly. "There shouldn't be anything on that frequency. It's crazy."

"Is it? I'm not sure," said Thor. "You say that the

73

wavelength is wrong?" Nigel nodded. "That fits in, I think. It looks as though Basil is starting to distort space-time itself."

Scott looked across in amazement. "Distort space-time?"

"That's what a full-scale black hole will do," said Thor. "If Basil's grown enough to start that sort of trouble, he's well and truly on the war-path. Here's a course for you. It may not be accurate, but I don't think it's far wrong. Don't trust the instruments, though, because they may be affected as well."

Scott shook his head in bewilderment, but he manœuvred the ferry until it was flying along the orbit Thor had given. Twice more they passed over the night-side of the earth, and each time they could see the glare coming from what they now believed to be tremendous fires, but there was no sign of the black hole itself, and at last Scott gave a grunt of relief; there was Station One, and Sir Eustace's voice came through the radio above the background hiss. "We're tracking you, but the radar is haywire, to put it mildly, and we've had another spot of bother here. Are you undamaged?"

"We're fine. Docking as soon as we can."

Actually it was a further half-hour before the ferry glided up to the port; the locking mechanism clicked home, and Scott switched off, rubbing his eyes thankfully. "That was tough going. Whew! I'm all in."

"That goes for me too," said Nigel heartily. "I hope it was worth it."

It was good to be back inside the Station; Peter Monk met them as soon as they came through the airlock, and with him was Gregory Voronov. Monk looked worried and anxious. "My dear fellows! We lost contact with you almost as soon as you left, and we've been completely out of touch."

"Station Three has been hit," said Gregory in a grim tone. "We're going to have to abandon the whole base, I think."

"Abandon the base?"

"Don't stand there chattering," barked Vale, swinging along the corridor in a series of leaps. "Thor, I want those pictures. How near did you get? Oh, no matter—they'll tell me all I want to know. Bring them down, and we'll develop them."

Thor followed without answering, and Scott looked at Gregory in bewilderment. "I don't get it," he said. "What do you mean about junking Station Three? Was it a bad hole?"

"Not particularly, but we haven't enough thrust to change our orbit by more than a few kilometres, and so far as we can tell we're right in the track of the black hole," said Gregory. "If it gets too close, it—well, it will break us up, I suppose. That's what the astronomers say, and they ought to know."

Monk gave a baffled gesture. "It makes no sense. One cannot send a shock-wave through space," he said, "and yet that is what seems to be happening. It must be some remarkable kind of distortion, but I simply cannot understand it. You look really ill, my dear fellows. Surely you should take some rest while you can?"

"Fat chance of that," grunted Nigel, though he had

to admit to himself that he felt all-in. "I could do with a bite, though. I'm starving."

Fussily, and in his usual bird-like manner, Monk ushered Scott and Nigel through to the main part of the Station, and insisted that they should have something to eat and drink. Scott at least was too tired to care. "Any idea what Reggie's up to?" he said gloomily. "I'd almost as soon tackle Carl Brand as our friend Basil, and that's saying something."

"I wish I could tell you. Are you sure that you are all right? If so, I will return to the observatory," said Monk. "Please join me if you wish."

He went out, and Scott stretched himself wearily; he had an overpowering desire to go to sleep, but he forced himself to concentrate. Presently Thomson's voice came over the Tannoy. "Commander to Saunders and Lorrimer. Report to Control Room immediately. Out."

Scott and Nigel lost no time. When they reached the control room they were not surprised to find that most of the senior crew members were there; Thomson himself, Vale and Sir Eustace, as well as Constantine Londos and half a dozen others. Noreiga and Maramoto were standing quietly by, looking as expressionless as usual. Vale looked up. "Let's have your report, please."

Scott gave a brief account of what had happened. He had just finished when Thor came in, carrying a pile of photographic plates. "Very much as we'd expected," he said. "Here you are."

Vale almost snatched the plates, and glared at them fiercely. Then he gave a shrug. "Quite so. The black hole has passed its critical size, and unless we manage to stop it there's nothing to prevent it from going on spreading. Confound it all! I'm starting to think that I'm beaten."

"Not yet," said Maramoto calmly. "We have a plan, remember."

"Plan! Don't be ridiculous." Vale gave a mirthless laugh. "Oh, I know it might work in theory, but there's no man who could last out for long enough to carry it through. Talk sense."

"We will try—" began Noreiga.

"Utter nonsense. It's impossible," said Vale curtly. "If I thought there was the slightest chance of success I'd go myself, and nobody would stop me, but the chances aren't even a million to one against. They're nil. Absolutely nil!"

There was a pause. "What do you mean?" asked Scott. "You must have got something up your sleeve."

Vale shook his head. "I tell you I'm beaten, and that's all there is to it."

"Steady, my dear chap," protested Sir Eustace; as usual, he was in full control of himself, and Vale made a visible effort to calm down. "You've been telling me all sorts of things I didn't know, but I wouldn't say that Basil has won the game yet, nasty specimen though he undoubtedly is. Go through it again, will you? Remember, I'm very stupid and dim-witted, and I may have missed something."

"I've told you all I can," said Vale wearily. "There may be a way of destroying this infernal thing, but I haven't any clue as to how to get near enough to try it, and nobody would have any hope of escaping. It would be straight suicide, and it wouldn't do any good in the end."

"Tell me," repeated Sir Eustace.

Vale shrugged. "All right, then. I suppose it may help me to clear my own brain—heaven knows, it's pretty well fuddled at the moment." He paused. "You know what a black hole is. Right in the middle of it there's a piece of super-dense material, pulling strongly enough to distort space and time. Within a certain distance—inside the boundary, or event horizon—the pull is so tremendous that not even light can get away, which is why that particular part of the universe is cut off from everything outside. Each time a new piece of material is sucked in, the black hole gets bigger and more powerful. If we could find a way to destroy the central lump, the whole thing might evaporate, and I believe that if we could send in a pulse of energy at sufficient strength we might do the trick. But—" again Vale paused—"to do that, we have to penetrate the black hole itself. No machine can have any chance at all, and a man would be ripped to pieces as soon as he went over the event horizon. That's what I mean by being beaten, and I'm bound to admit it."

Sir Eustace nodded. "Hmm. Very difficult. You mean that someone has got to break right into the black hole?"

"That's what I said. There's no hard, visible boundary, but we know where the event horizon is, because the atoms being sucked in are whirled about and heated so violently that they glow and send out X-rays. We've proved that," said Vale. "Unfortunately, no flesh and blood could stand the strain, and transmitting the energy-beam from outside is no use, because it couldn't get through. Now do you see the problem?"

"I do," agreed Sir Eustace. "It doesn't seem easy, but I still have a feeling that there must be a way out—or rather, in. I know you've both volunteered to try it," he added as Noreiga began to speak, "and I'm lost in admiration, but so far as I can see it would be rather more fatal than putting your heads inside a gas-oven, and that woulddn't do anybody any good."

Scott gave a sudden gasp, and jumped forward. "I —I wonder. It could work. I'm sure it could!"

Vale stared. "What the blazes are you jabbering about?"

Scott breathed hard. "I'm not jabbering," he said steadily. "Listen. You said that no flesh and blood could stand going inside the hole, didn't you?" Vale nodded. "All right, then. I believe I know someone who'd be able to pull it off."

"You idiot!" Vale gave an exclamation of annoyance. "Don't waste our time. Have a little sense!"

"I'm not fooling," said Scott, and looked across at Sir Eustace. "I told you I knew someone who could see it through, and I'm right. I must be right."

Sir Eustace raised his eyebrows. "I'd be the last to accuse you of going off your chump, but you must admit that it seems a little odd. Who is this interesting character? Superman?"

Scott gave a grin. "Not far off, if you only knew it. He's just the chap we want. His name's Robbie."

Chapter 7

INTO THE UNKNOWN

Sir Eustace Wainwright rubbed his moustache, and looked puzzled. "Robbie?" he repeated. "I thought I knew most people, either by name or by reputation, but I'm afraid I'm floundering. Do please explain, before I resign myself to being carted off to a padded cell." He paused, and then drew in his breath. "Ah. I begin to see. Very clever."

"You've got it," said Scott steadily. "When we were over on the moon with Dr. Lang, he showed us what he'd been doing. Robbie's a robot, all right, but he looks like a man, and he's got a brain of sorts. He could be programmed to take a rocket right in—at least, I reckon he could—and he could go on functioning a lot longer than any of us."

"And I call myself a scientist," said Vale in a disgusted tone. "I'm sorry, young Scott; you've a great deal more sense than I have. It just might be the answer . . . ." He turned to Noreiga. "I gave up too early. We're not beaten yet."

"Excellent," said Sir Eustace cheerfully. "More power to your elbow, my dear Reggie. If you really think this scheme is good enough to be given a whirl, to use an old-fashioned expression, we'd better cut the cackle and get busy before Basil becomes too much for even our Mr. Robbie to handle."

"Not so fast," broke in Thomson. "Even if Lang can produce this robot of his, we'll need to bring it across from the moon—"

"Not 'it', my dear Richard. 'Him'," said Sir Eustace. "I haven't had the pleasure of meeting him yet, of course, but he sounds a most interesting lad. May I ask how far his education goes? I mean, can he play the violin and recite Shakespearean sonnets, or can he just say 'Ug' and 'Og'?"

Nigel managed to chuckle, though he did not feel at all like laughing; somehow Sir Eustace always succeeded in making a crisis seem trivial. "He's quite a chatterbox, but whether he's going to be able to cope with electronics I don't know. I reckon it'll depend on his teacher."

Vale straightened up. "It may or may not be a mad scheme, but I can't think of a better one, so we'll do our best. The first thing to do is to call Lang; if we can't get through by radio we'll have to send a ferry, which will waste more time than we can afford. Noreiga, you and Maramoto had better start working on a computer programme; it'll be largely guesswork until we know how complicated the robot's circuits are, but it'll be a start. I'll work with Thor on the actual energy projector. Confound it, we need at least a month, and we haven't got more than a few hours." He looked at Scott and Nigel. "I'm ordering you two to bed. You're useless for the moment, but you may be very useful indeed when the time comes."

"We—" began Scott.

Vale broke in. "I told you to go to bed. Don't argue, or I'll tell Constantine to give you a sleeping tablet that will knock you out well and truly. I want you fresh and alert, not yawning your stupid heads off. Understand?"

"I reckon so," said Scott quietly. "We're the flyers, is that it?"

"I don't know what the situation will be, but we've got to be ready, and unfortunately I'd rather have you two young idiots with me than anyone else," said Vale shortly, and turned away. "You've had your orders."

It seemed strange to be going quietly to sleep as though nothing were happening. Scott could hardly believe that not far away from them, one of the most dangerous forces in the universe was gathering strength; but he was almost at the end of his reserves, and both he and Nigel were inwardly glad of the chance to stretch themselves out in the bedroom that they shared. Beds were of no practical use in a space-station, where there was no feeling of weight, but after years of experience they were used to the conditions, and on the whole they felt much more comfortable than they did on the rare occasions when they went down either to the earth or the moon. Scott yawned. "Boy! I guess I could sleep for a week. Think old Robbie will come up to scratch?"

"He may have been dismantled for all we know," said Nigel gloomily. "He was only No. 1 in the experiment, and I don't know if Homer Lang meant to keep him going for long."

"You are a cheerful bloke! Let's hope Robbie's rarin' to go," said Scott as lightly as he could. "Right."

It was not long before he slept, and it seemed only a few minutes before he felt himself being shaken. "Up you get," said Nigel. "Didn't you hear that call?"

"What call? Phew, I'm all woozy." Scott rubbed his eyes. "Don't tell me we're in for a trip to the moon?"

"No, thank goodness. Robbie's on his way," said Nigel. "Dr. Lang said he'd be here any time, so we'd better be on our toes. Wakey-wakey!"

Scott shook himself, and pulled on his clothes; washing was something that could wait. "Basil's still on the rampage, I suppose. I don't envy the Russians over in Station Three."

"They've got clear," said Nigel. "From what Gregory says, Three's in pretty bad shape even though Basil hasn't bashed into it. There's trouble all over earth, too."

"What sort of trouble?"

"More or less what you'd expect. We were right about those fires in Australia. There was a terrific storm that caught the flames and spread them around like nobody's business, and there were tidal waves as well. The United Nations has called what they call a 'global state of emergency'," said Nigel. "I've just been looking at some of the pictures on TV. They're fantastic."

Scott looked grim. "Many people killed?"

"Can't say, but it looks rather like it. The TV went

blank before we'd got the full story. Come on," said Nigel impatiently. "I want to be around when Robbie arrives."

Scott was wide awake now, but it was another half-hour before Homer Lang managed to make contact, and the time dragged. Scott wandered into the communications room, and for a few minutes some blurred pictures were visible on the television screen; the Australian bush fires were even worse than he had feared, and there were brief views of the devastation caused by the hurricane-force winds sweeping over Asia and North America. London had not escaped. There, too, a violent gale had blown down many of the buildings that had been standing for hundreds of years, and there was a sad picture of Nelson's Column lying prone across Trafalgar Square. Also, there was the almost complete destruction of Station Three. Mercifully there had been no casualties, but it was painfully clear that the Station was a wreck. "It will take years to repair," said Gregory Voronov miserably. "It was my home— and look at it now!"

At last Thor Eiriksson came in, his eyes red-rimmed and his hair tousled. "I've got to have a bit of rest. I've been working with Reggie all the time you two were snoring, and I'm done in. So's Reggie, for that matter."

"I'm not surprised," said Nigel. "Point is, have you got anywhere?"

"I think so, but it all depends on Robbie the Robot. Dr. Lang came through just now. He'll be docking within the next ten minutes."

Scott and Nigel made their way to the docking port at the far end of Station One, and waited expectantly; Gregory joined them, together with Thomson and a weary-looking Maramoto. "We are to blame for all this," said Maramoto in a low voice. "We have been very stupid, I fear. We will never forgive ourselves."

"There's one thing," said Nigel. "What was the idea of the experiment in the first place? Making super-dense material doesn't seem very useful to me."

"Perhaps not, but we are physicists; we are seeking new knowledge, and we hoped that our work would be of great value." Maramoto sighed. "We could not foresee this terrible mistake . . . Look. There is a ferry. I will call Dr. Vale."

By the time Vale reached the airlock, the ferry was close in, and Homer Lang's voice came through the radio; the rocket docked, and the airlocks connecting it with the Station clicked shut. Lang came out, unfastening his clumsy helmet, and he was followed by a figure which was so strikingly human that Scott has to force himself to remember that it was made of metal. "Hallo," he said, feeling rather foolish. "Hallo, Robbie!"

The robot's mouth opened. "I greet you, friend. I greet you."

"He's learned a lot since you last saw him," said Lang, "and I guess that's just as well. I don't know what you want, Reggie, but I've done as you asked me."

"Bring him in," said Vale curtly. "I'll explain while we work. I gather you know the latest news?" Lang gave a nod. "The black hole's swelling quickly, and before long it will be impossible to send any radio signals at all, because the distortion in space-time will make it hopeless. Come with me, please. No, I don't want you yet awhile," he added to Scott and Nigel, "and if you blunder about in the laboratory you'll only get in the way. Stay either in the control room or in the observatory, and wait until I call you."

"It's uncanny," muttered Thomson, gazing at Robbie as though hypnotized. "You're telling me that —that the thing's really got a brain?"

"Sure depends on what you call a brain. He's no slouch," said Homer Lang, "but we're only at an early stage, and so far he's the only one of his breed. This way, Robbie."

Scott and Nigel were too wise to argue with Vale in this mood. Thor followed them back into the main part of the Station, and then made for his room. "I'll get a bit of sleep, but I'll wake up as soon as I'm wanted. I've done all I can for the moment."

By now the television was almost useless, and the occasional flashes that came through were so blurred and unsteady that nothing could be learned from them. Thomson tried the radio, but here too the interference was impossibly strong. "We're out of touch," he said at last, "but the last message I did pick up wasn't very encouraging. The storms are spreading all over the globe, and there's no sign of any let-up."

"It's all very annoying," agreed Sir Eustace, staring at the blank screen as though it were deliberately misleading him. "From what I can gather from our scientific friends, Basil's playing havoc with the atmosphere in some way, and nobody seems to have any idea of how to cope with him. He's changed his orbit, too, and he's coming downwards."

"You don't mean there's anyone guiding it?" muttered Nigel.

"I would say that anything of the sort is most unlikely. Even Carl Brand and his merry men couldn't do it," said Sir Eustace. "No, the snag is that Basil's mass —his weight, if you like—is getting greater and greater, and that affects the way in which he moves. Frankly, I dislike the entire situation."

"Don't we all?" grunted Nigel. "It's up to Robbie now, I suppose."

"Robbie can't do much on his own," said Thomson curtly, "and it would be idiotic to place too much faith in him. Remember, he's only a machine, even though he does look almost human, and he can't think for himself."

The wait seemed endless. Twice the Station shifted slightly, and Scott had the feeling that some tremendous outside force was acting on it, but then the vibration ceased. Presently he went over to the observatory, but for once Monk and Santos were not there; the main telescope was still out of action, and Scott could do no more than look at the stars through the transparent dome, searching for the tell-tale glow marking the boundary of the black hole. At last he heard his name being called, and he almost raced back to the laboratory, swinging himself along in the way he had learned during his time in space.

The laboratory was a typically untidy place. Vale always boasted that he knew every piece of apparatus better than the back of his hand, but to anyone else the scene appeared to be chaotic. It was even more so now; Nigel, Thor and Vale were all there, as well as Lang and the two Japanese. "Reporting for duty," said Scott. "What's up?"

"A great deal. I'd better explain," said Vale; his voice was low and controlled, quite unlike his usual brusqueness. "I'll tell you what I have in mind, and if you don't feel like tackling it, I'll be the last to blame you. Listen carefully." Scott nodded. "I'll have to give you a bit of a lecture—you too, Nigel—because unless you really understand the problem, you'll be quite unprepared to cope with it."

"We're listening," said Nigel.

"Very well. This is the situation." Vale paused. "As you know, the one hope, so far as I can see, is to penetrate the black hole itself. If we can send a tremendous pulse of energy into the chunk of stuff in the middle, we may destroy it—literally make it crush itself out of existence, in which case I believe the black hole will vanish too. Shooting the energy-beam from outside is no good, because it can't penetrate the event horizon. That means that there's got to be a pilot."

"Robbie," said Scott softly.

"Yes, but unfortunately the robot has its limitations. As Homer told you, it's a prototype—the first of its kind, and it's still pretty elementary. We've made some makeshift additions to its brain-circuits, if you can call them that, but we can't make the electronics complicated enough to do the whole job. Neither can we set the sequence up until the very last moment. Understand?"

"I think so," said Scott uncertainly.

"Very well, then. This is the plan," said Vale. "We've got two ferries fully equipped with my protective screen; without that we couldn't get within range at all, partly because of these extraordinary shockwaves and partly because of the X-radiation that is being sent out. I'll go in one of them, together with Robbie. I'll get in as close as I can, and then I'll activate the robot brain. With luck, he'll do the rest. The power can't last for more than a few minutes, but it should be enough." He paused. "If I stay on board, I'll be dead the instant we go through the event horizon. That's something I'm prepared to face if I have to, but it all depends on whether anyone else has the nerve to come in the second ferry and try to get me out."

"Let me speak," interrupted Noreiga, his tone quite unlike its usual bland flatness. "Dr. Vale is right, because only he has the skill to complete the final programme of the robot, and not even Dr. Lang could do it. Professor Maramoto and I have already said that we will take the second ferry. It is true that we are not clever pilots, but we will do our best."

"And scupper the lot of you?" said Scott, and looked at Nigel. "This is our job. We're with you."

Vale breathed hard. "That wasn't my idea, and I

know I've no right to bring you two lads into danger like that. I'll make it on my own."

"You won't," said Scott steadily, "and you know it. We're coming with you, and you're not going to stop us!"

Chapter 8

NIGHTMARE JOURNEY

Noreiga broke the long silence. "You are very brave," he said. "Yes, you are very brave, but it must not be so. It is a task for Professor Maramoto and myself. We have been the cause of this tragedy, and it is only right that we should make amends if it lies within our power to do so."

Nigel forced a grin. "Not likely, sir. You admit that you aren't clever pilots. What good will it do if you get out there and can't handle the ferry? That's where we come in."

"I agree," said Thor quietly. "I will come also."

"You've always said that we were pretty good flyers," said Scott. "Now's our chance to show it. If anyone can haul you out of the mess, we can."

"I know that perfectly well," said Vale. "As I've said before, if I'm in a tight corner there are only three people I'd want with me—but this is different. You'd be risking your necks to save mine, and that isn't a fair deal."

"It is. What's the sense of arguing? You know we're coming," said Scott. "We're pretty tough, even if Basil is a lot bigger and heavier than we are."

Vale turned away. "I know that I couldn't stop you

even if I tried, and there's nothing I can say. We'll save the chat till later. I'm blasting off as soon as I've finished checking the robot's circuits."

Scott glanced at Robbie; he had not realized that the robot was in the laboratory. "You're ready, then?"

"I am ready," came the strange metallic voice. "I am at your service."

"It's weird," muttered Nigel. "Are you dead sure he can't think for himself?"

"Don't be absurd," said Vale roughly. "I tell you its a machine, and it doesn't matter whether it looks like a man or like a dustbin—except that in operating the controls of a ferry it's just as well to have arms and legs. We'll be as quick as we can."

For some time Scott and Nigel watched the scientists at work. Robbie's head was made in two halves, and when the back portion was raised all the wires and terminals were visible; Scott wondered stupidly whether the robot could feel any pain, but then shook himself angrily. "I'm letting my nerves fool me," he thought. "Pull yourself together, you clot!"

Presently Thor came over. "My job's going to be handling the electronics," he said. "That means I'll be going along in Rocket No. 1. Reggie could do it on his own, but it'll be better with two. We'll have quite a crowd on our way back."

"If we get back," said Nigel, with a wry grin. "See here, you're one of the brains of this outfit. Isn't there some guff about time being warped as well as space? Darned if I want to blast off and come back in the Stone Age!"

The Icelandic boy grinned back. "True enough, but you needn't worry about being eaten by dinosaurs. Travelling backwards in time is one of the few things that's really impossible. In any case, these weird effects don't start making themselves felt except when the gravitational pull is really enormous, and Basil isn't as massive as that—not yet, at least." Thor paused. "On the other hand, none of us can tell just what will happen when we get close to the event horizon."

"Event horizon . . . that's the edge of the black hole," said Scott. "Once on the other side of that, we'd never get out."

"We're not going over. That's up to Robbie," said Thor. "You'd better go and get something to eat. You can't be of any help here, and there's a pretty hectic time ahead of us."

Neither Scott nor Nigel felt like eating, and more by force of habit than anything else they wandered back to the observatory. Santos was busy at the telescope, but he had nothing to add to what they already knew, and for once he was not in a talkative mood. "Everything is wrong," he said. "The stars, the sun, the earth —I am confused, you understand."

"What about the X-rays?"

"They are strong. Indeed, they are a cause of danger," said Santos. "I am not happy, my friends."

"Neither are we," said Scott. "Be seeing you, Juan."

The radio was still useless; Thomson was alone in the control room. "I was just going to send for you," he said, as Scott and Nigel came in; the base commander looked pale and tired, and his voice was strained. "You're sure about this?"

"Think we'd let Reggie and Thor go on their own?" said Nigel, as confidently as he could. "That's not on!"

Thomson nodded. "I knew what your answer would be, but I had to ask you. I only wish I could help, but a cripple wouldn't be much use out there." It was seldom that the base commander mentioned his disability, and that alone showed that he was desperately worried. "We've done all we can, and—well, all I can say is 'good luck'. You'd better go over to the docking port. I've had the ferry checked, of course, but you may want to have a look at it yourselves."

Vale was waiting for them, Thor by his side. "Ready," said Vale, as calmly as though he were organizing a trip to the seaside. "Robbie's in our rocket, all wired up; he knows what he's got to do, and as soon as I give the word he'll start going through his programme. If we haven't joined up any of his circuits the wrong way, he ought to last for long enough to break through the event horizon; after that nobody can tell what will happen. Scott, you'll pilot the second ferry; Nigel, keep on the radio and do your best to keep in touch, though I doubt if you'll have much chance of success. There's one thing more," he added. "If Thor and I run into real trouble, don't hang around waiting for us. Blast away, and get out as quickly as you can. Is that clear?"

"Clear as mud," said Scott, and Vale glared. "You'll do exactly as you're told. Stop talking like an imbecile, and get ready to blast off." He handed over a slip of paper. "This is the orbit."

Scott nodded. "Understood. How's Robbie?"

"We've built as much into him as we can," said Thor. "It was a rush job, and we can't be sure we haven't made any mistakes, but we're hoping for the best. If he can keep on working for thirty seconds after he takes over, he'll have done his job."

"He won't come back, then," said Scott thoughtfully. "Seems a bit rough, doesn't it?"

"Oh, for heaven's sake!" roared Vale. "What do you take him for—a pet poodle? If you've any stupid ideas about him, you can forget them. Get busy."

Somehow Scott would have liked to take a last look at the robot, presumably now strapped down in the ferry and just starting on a mission which he could not hope to survive, but he had the tact to say no more, and he swung himself into the pilot's couch. Nigel followed, and the airlock slammed shut. "Ferry to Base," said Nigel into the transmitter. "We are ready to take off. Permission to undock."

The headphones crackled. "Have a nice time," said Sir Eustace. "If I wasn't so ancient and stupid I'd be right with you, and you know it. We'll keep in contact as long as we can. Off you go—and give my love to Basil if you get within range."

Scott was in no way deceived; he knew just what Sir Eustace was going through. "So-long," he said lightly. "Be seeing you."

Cautiously he switched on, and the motors came to life; the rocket undocked with the usual soft jerk, and then it was clear of Station One, floating gently away into the darkness of space. Nigel concentrated on the radio, and managed to pick up Vale's voice: "We're undocked. Set course, and keep as close to me as you can. The one thing we mustn't do is to get separated."

Scott set his jaw, and studied the slip of paper that Vale had given him. Normally a trip of this length would have been child's play, but within ten minutes he knew that things were far from normal. The instruments were not reliable; they swung aimlessly around, and Scott realized that he would have to navigate more or less by instinct. "I've lost touch," said Nigel gloomily. "All I can hear is a hiss like a thousand snakes. How're you doing, pal?"

"I can see Reggie's ferry, but that's about all," muttered Scott. "I've sighted one of the other stations— I think it's Five—but otherwise I'm just doing my best to keep Reggie in view. For Pete's sake get me a radar fix on him if you can."

"No go. Radar's out of action. Sorry," said Nigel. "Look down there. More fires!"

Scott glanced down at the surface of the earth, far below; again he could see that unpleasant glow, and he shivered. "It's up to us, I reckon. If Basil can cause this sort of damage when he's still small, just think of what he'll be able to do when he swells out. I—I don't believe we've a hope."

"Don't talk rot," said Nigel stoutly. "Reggie isn't licked yet, and neither is Robbie."

Scott said no more; he concentrated upon piloting the ferry, though in fact there was not much to do except when a course alteration had to be made, and his main task was to keep close to Vale. The two rockets were no more than a mile apart, travelling in the same direction at the same rate, but several times Vale gave a burst of power to increase his height above ground level, and Scott followed suit. Three times they came over the sunlit side of the earth, and then plunged back into comparative darkness, but still there was no sign of the black hole, and the ferry stayed perfectly steady. "Wonder if we've mucked it up," was the thought that flashed through Scott's mind. "If so, we'll run out of power before we can do much—"

Nigel broke in. "Hold on, pal. I can hear Thor." He paused. "Yes—it's him. Message says they've sighted Basil, and they're starting the run-in. Ready?"

"As ready as I'll ever be," said Scott dryly. "Here goes."

It was a nerve-racking period. Scott had never tried this sort of hit-or-miss space navigation before; he had no planned orbit, and he had to use the rocket motors to keep the ferry within striking distance of the speck of light that was Vale's craft. Then he saw something else. It was a glow, much larger than it had been before, with the flashing and sparking even more noticeable. "There it is," breathed Nigel, from the observation window. "That's Basil. Boy, has he grown!"

"Screen on," said Scott steadily.

"Going at full blast. If it wasn't, we'd be in the cart; I bet Basil's sending out a whole flood of his pet X-rays," said Nigel. "Phew! I'm sweating! How near do you reckon Reggie's going to get?"

"Haven't a clue. Try and call him," said Scott. "He may be able to hear us, even if we can't hear him. Worth having a shot."

Nigel eased himself back to the radio desk, and spoke slowly and clearly into the microphone, but there was no response apart from the all too familiar hiss. "No go. Better start closing in."

The eerie glow was brilliant now, and Scott fancied that he could almost hear the crackling as the boundary of the black patch flashed and sparked. He risked accelerating, and Vale's ferry became brighter. As the two rockets closed in, the blue radiance flooded through the observation window, almost blinding him; he pulled down his protective goggles, and clamped his hands on the controls, but next moment there was a lurch that threw him sideways, and he tightened the straps holding him down on his couch. "Getting hot," he breathed. "For Pete's sake keep the screen running. We can't be far from the edge—"

He broke off with a gasp of dismay. Ahead of him, still clear of the blue glow, he could see that something was happening to Vale's ferry. It was no longer steady; it was weaving its way along, and it looked as though it had gone out of control. "They're in trouble," he said hoarsely. "We'll have to go in."

"Message coming through," rapped Nigel. "I can hear them. It's Thor—he's telling us to go back."

"Not on your life. In we go!"

"Wait," shouted Nigel. "I can't hear what they're saying—no, that's Thor. He's telling us they've got too close. See if you can make it out!"

Scott switched on his receiver, and winced as the deafening hiss filled his eardrums. Then he could distinguish a voice that could only be Vale's "We can't get free. I'm going to start Robbie's programme—we'll get through the event horizon, and Robbie may last long enough to fire the energy-beam. Nothing you can do. Get clear!"

"Stop it," roared Scott at the top of his voice. "We're coming to get you. Hold on—we're on our way!"

This time it was Thor who answered. "Get back, I tell you. We've lost our power, and we're having to use the screen transmitters to feed into Robbie's brain. It's the last hope."

Scott twisted his head round to Nigel. "O.K. to go in?"

Nigel nodded, and Scott did not hesitate. Again he fired the motors, and the ferry accelerated, slowly and jerkily as though being pounded with an iron bar; Scott wrestled with the controls, and managed to keep on course. Now they were almost up to Vale's ferry, but the light ahead was dazzling, and beyond there was nothing but an ocean of blackness. "Get ready," said Nigel into the transmitter. "Our motors are still working. Get ready."

There was no answer, and the lurching and jolting had become so violent that Scott felt sick, but even at that moment he had no thought of turning back. "I'll have to go out," he said thickly. "Can you take her? I'll see if I can get them—"

"You're mad," panted Nigel. "You won't have a hope. We're slap in the middle of the X-rays—"

99

"I know, but I'll have to chance it. Take over!"

Scott plunged toward the airlock, and Nigel swung into the pilot's couch. Somehow Scott forced the inner door open; it was dark inside the tiny lock, and the jolting and pitching was almost unbearable. "I'm going through. Tell them I'm on my way. Quick."

He operated the outer lock, and the door swung slowly back; Scott was in outer space, and the sight was something beyond his wildest dreams. Ahead of him he could see Vale's rocket, but beyond was the intense bluish glare that he had come to dread, and inside it there was—nothing. Scott turned away, and to his immense relief saw the airlock of the second ferry was open. "Reggie—Thor! Now!"

He fired the small but powerful suit-motor, and manoeuvred himself toward the rocket airlock. Next moment he was through, and he gave a shout. "You young fool," he heard Vale say. "Get back, while there's still time!"

Scott steadied himself. The cabin was in a state of wild disorder, but Robbie was still in the pilot's couch, as expressionless as ever. "Get into the lock," said Scott swiftly. "We'll make it, but hurry!"

Vale swung round. "Out you go, Thor. This is up to me." He staggered as another blow struck the ferry. "I know what I'm doing. Get out, and let me start the programme."

Thor plunged into the airlock. Scott hesitated; he saw Vale swing over to the motionless robot, and fumble with the switches in the strangely human head. Then he was thrust roughly backwards into the lock.

"It's started," rapped Vale. "Back, for your life. We've got less than a minute."

Scott could not reply; Vale propelled him outward, and almost before he knew it he was back in the air-lock of his own ferry. Next moment he was inside, and Nigel turned. "Can't use the motors. They're dead," he said flatly. "We're being sucked in. It's all up!"

Scott never forgot the next few seconds. The pitching and lurching had almost stopped, but the blue glow was so intense that he could not look at it; then he saw Vale point. "There it goes. We may have done the trick after all. Wait!"

Scott gulped. There was a strange calm now; the glow seemed to be all round them, while ahead there was a gulf of darkness more intense than anything he had seen before. There, too, was the other ferry, pre-sumably with Robbie at the controls, moving slowly but steadily toward the black patch. "Wonder what Robbie's doing," thought Scott stupidly, and braced himself, expecting every moment to be hurled into eternity.

"It's going in," breathed Vale. "If he gets inside, and if he lasts long enough to fire the ray—"

Now the ferry was almost at the edge of the black-ness; for an instant it flickered, and then it vanished. Next moment there came a blaze of light, and the ferry was thrown back with a last, sickening jolt. Scott lost his balance; he was hurled across the cabin, and he felt a blur of pain as his head struck the outer wall. A red mist swirled in front of his eyes, and everything faded out.

Chapter 9

ALIEN UNIVERSE

Slowly and painfully Scott came round. His head throbbed, and he felt blood on his face; everything was pitch dark, and he blinked his eyes open. "Phew! Where—where are we?"

For a moment there was no answer, and Scott felt a surge of panic. Then he heard Nigel's voice. "We're here, but we can't see a thing. Lights aren't working."

The darkness was complete, and Scott struggled toward the observation window, feeling about with his hands. Yes—there was the window, but no light came through. "It's crazy," he heard Thor say. "The sun's gone out. It must have done!"

"Don't be absurd!" Scott was glad to hear Vale's usual sharp tone. "I don't know what is going on, but we'll soon find out." A flashlight beam pierced the darkness. "There must be trouble with the power circuits, I suppose, but I've no doubt that I can fix it. Stay where you are, and don't start blundering around."

Scott relaxed; at least they were alive, even though they were hopelessly cut off from earth as well as the orbital stations. But what about the darkness? In space, there was always a certain amount of light coming through the observation window of a rocket; there were the stars, the moon, the earth, and—of course—the sun. Yet at the moment nothing could be seen, and he shook himself. "Must be that we're simply facing the wrong way," he told himself, but inwardly he was becoming more and more apprehensive.

Minutes passed, and then, suddenly, the cabin lights came on. "Just as I thought," said Vale. "It was nothing more nor less than a broken connection. Well, now we can start doing some investigations."

The cabin looked as though a bomb had hit it. All kinds of odds and ends were floating around, and one of the main panels had been wrenched away; evidently the shock had been even greater than Scott had realized. Nigel had a deep cut in his temple, and both Vale and Thor were bruised and shaken. "I didn't like that," said Nigel breathlessly. "What the blazes was it?"

"If I knew that, I'd be a great deal happier than I am," said Vale dryly. "At this moment your guess is as good as mine, which isn't saying much. What bothers me most is the lack of light. It doesn't make any sense at all, and I admit that I've no idea where we are."

"But—" Scott looked at him curiously. "Hang it all, we must be in the same place as we were before the bang. We can't have been blasted out of earth orbit."

"I have an unpleasant feeling that it may be more sinister than that," said Vale, "but I may be making a fool of myself, so we'll have to do our best to find out. Try the motors."

Nigel switched on. Nothing happened, and he shook his head. "Still dead," he said slowly. "Not a squeak out of them. Must have been damaged when we were hit by—well, whatever it was."

Vale inspected the panel. "The protective screen isn't working, either," he muttered. "This is getting more and more peculiar. We're not accelerating, so we're not being pulled out of orbit by a black hole or anything else—and come to that, where's the black hole itself?"

"We can't be anywhere near it," said Thor. "We'd see the glare."

"Quite so." Vale allowed himself to float clear of the cabin wall. "I'm prepared to bet that the radio is dead too, in which case we're cut off from everyone."

Nigel nodded. "Right. I can't even hear a crackle—I just don't know what to make of it. Listen."

Scott took a pair of headphones, and rammed them into position; Vale and Thor followed suit. Generally there was always a good deal of background hiss, but now there was utter silence. Nothing came through, and Scott shook his head in bewilderment. Nigel sent a call: "Ferry to Base. Ferry to Base. Answer!" but there was no reply.

Vale took off his headphones. "No light, no radio, no sun. Either we're all crazy, or else we've blundered into something beyond any human experience," he said quietly. "There's one way to find out. I'm going to take a space-walk."

"Go outside?" said Scott.

Vale nodded. "No reason why I shouldn't. The one good thing about this is that we don't seem to have been damaged, apart from the lack of rocket power, and so far we've plenty of oxygen, so we're safe for the moment. Come with me, if you like. In fact, it may be as well if you do."

"And me," said Nigel, but Vale shook his head. "Not more than two at a time, I think. Remember that we may have no thrust from our suit-motors either; if we're in the middle of a strong interference-field they may be as dead as the main engines, and we'll have to make very sure that our safety-lines are fixed. Get ready, Scott."

Scott wiped the blood from his face, and crammed himself into the familiar vacuum-suit. Carefully he checked the oxygen tank, and switched on the transmitter in his helmet. "Seems all right," he said. "Let's go."

Vale operated the inner door, and stepped into the airlock; Scott followed, and the door swung shut. There was a pause as the air in the tiny compartment was drawn back into the cabin, and then Vale went to the outer door. "We may be in for a shock," he said quietly. "It could be the strangest moment of your life, young Scott. Don't say I didn't warn you."

Scott clenched his teeth, and watched as the outer door slid gently back. "What do you mean?"

"You'll understand soon enough, if I'm on the right track," said Vale. "Follow me, and make absolutely sure that you don't lose your safety-line. If you drift away in this murk, there'll be no possible way of finding you again."

He went through the airlock; Scott followed—and gave a cry of amazement. "There's nothing here," he whispered. "Reggie, there's nothing here. You're right —we must all be mad!"

"Look round," breathed Vale. "This is something I never expected to see—or rather, not to see. Uncanny!"

Scott stared first one way and then another. Absolutely nothing could be seen. There were no stars; there was no earth, and neither was there any sign of the sun, usually so brilliant that to look straight at it was to run the risk of serious eye damage. "What is it?" muttered Scott in a dazed voice. "It can't be true!"

Vale spun slowly round. "Just as I thought," he said. "Yes, there's only one answer to this . . . do you start to see what I mean?"

A voice came through the headphones, and Scott jumped. "What's it like, pal?" asked Nigel. "No chance of getting a star fix?"

"No stars to see," said Scott in a low voice. "There's nothing here, Nigel. It's just—black. We're alone in the universe!"

"You may be pretty near the truth," said Vale, and eased himself toward the ferry. "Better not try your suit motor, Scott. It might or might not work—on the whole, I think it wouldn't—but we're in a completely new dimension, and it's best not to take any unnecessary risks."

"A new dimension?" repeated Scott helplessly.

"That's what I said, and by now I'm almost sure that I'm right. Back into the lock, please. We can't do any good out here, and we've seen all we can."

Scott edged obediently toward the open airlock, and

then paused to take a last look round. Never before had there been such blackness; it seemed to crowd in on him, and he gave a shudder. "The sun," he said stupidly. "The sun. It can't have—well, it can't have gone out. That's too mad for words!"

"Inside," repeated Vale, and Scott hesitated no longer. The outer door slid to; air hissed back into the lock, and Scott stumbled back into the cabin. "All right," said Thor quietly. "We heard what you were saying. I believe I'm starting to see what's happened to us."

Vale took off his helmet. "I thought you'd tumble to it before long, but I wanted to be sure," he said. "What we're going to do about it is quite another matter, and one thing I can tell you straight away: there's no possible chance of anyone coming to our rescue. We've got to work this out for ourselves."

"I still don't get it," muttered Scott.

"I'll tell you, then. Listen," said Vale. "Just before that jolt, Robbie's ferry must have gone through the event horizon of the black hole. It can't have survived for more than a second at best, but if my calculations are right that should have been just enough time for the robot to fire the energy-ray. That's what I'd built into the circuits, and it seems to have worked, to some extent at least." He paused. "As I've told you, the black hole was caused by a tiny piece of super-dense matter right in its centre. The hole itself was only a few hundred yards wide, and the beam must have sliced straight across it. If it hit the centre, it would have crushed the material there right out of existence—or, alternatively, blasted it out of our own dimension into a completely separate universe. Unfortunately, we seem to have been blasted away with it."

Scott gasped. "You mean—"

"I mean that all those weird and wonderful theories about black holes have been correct," said Vale. "Remember them? 'Go into a black hole, and you'll come out in a different space-time'. It may have sounded gibberish, but there was always a chance that it was true, and even if we never get back we'll have the satisfaction of having proved it."

"What's the odds?" said Nigel, and stared out of the window into the blackness. "Does it mean that we're—well, does it mean that we're marooned?"

"At the moment, we certainly are. Ordinary material can't link up to two separate dimensions of space-time," said Vale curtly. "What we don't know, of course, is whether this new universe is empty or not, and neither have I any idea how far the effect will have stretched out. I'd say that all the bases were outside the danger-zone, but that's another thing I can't check at the moment."

There was a long silence, and Scott did his best to take a grip on himself. He was no coward, as he had shown time and time again since he had first gone into space; he was used to facing ordinary dangers, but this was something quite beyond his understanding, and he knew that he was as frightened as he had ever been in his life. Then Thor broke the silence. "If we can't use our rockets, we can't move," he said. "Not that it would help us if we could. We can't get anything out of the radio, and we can't see anything either. What do we do—wait here and hope that something will turn up?"

"I've no intention of sitting back and doing nothing, but I'll need time to think," said Vale. "Keep watching, all of you, and let me know if you see the slightest sign of a light. I'm going to go through the circuits, and see what I can make of them."

He went through into the propulsion room of the ferry, and Scott gave a slight shrug. "Even if Reggie could get the power going, what good would that do? We'd only start on a trip to nowhere," he said. "Pretty grim outlook, I reckon. We'll be darned lucky to come through this one." Then a sudden thought struck him. "Wonder what happened to Robbie?"

"Robbie will have been wiped out of existence as soon as the energy-pulse hit the black hole," said Thor. "He may have done his job first, but I don't expect we'll ever know."

Scott nodded. "I guess you're right. You know, I wish he'd got away with it!"

Nigel forced a grin. "You were getting quite pally with him, weren't you?"

"I know I'm a clot," said Scott, "and I know he was only a robot, but—well, he wasn't a bad old guy . . . We'd better keep listening out, I suppose, just in case anyone's able to call us. I'd be darned glad to hear anything, even if it's a bug-eyed monster."

"I've turned the receiver up to maximum, but it's dead quiet," said Nigel. "I don't believe there's anyone here. We've got a whole universe to ourselves."

Time passed, and then Scott gave a soft gasp. "Check

your watches," he said. "This is crazier than ever. They're—they're going backwards!"

Nigel and Thor looked down swiftly. "You're right," stammered Nigel. "Boy! that proves it. What did Reggie mean about a different sort of space-time?"

"Just what he said. We've left our own universe, and we're in a dimension where everything is reversed." Thor kept his eyes on the timepiece on his wrist. "We'd always thought that a black hole would cause a warp in space, if you can call it that, but—Look! Look there!"

Scott swung round to the window. "Where?"

Thor pointed. "A light of some sort. I can just about see it . . . No, it's gone. It just winked out."

"I saw it too," said Nigel, "but it wasn't a star; it was moving. Reggie, did you get it?"

"Of course I didn't," snapped Vale from the far end of the ferry. "I've been checking on the propulsion units to see if there's any way of getting them going. Try the radio."

Nigel obeyed. Again and again he called; still there was utter silence, until, suddenly, he heard something. "Listen out," he breathed. "May be a voice!"

Sure enough there was a faint murmur in the headphones, and Scott strained his ears, trying desperately to make out the words. Then he shook his head. "Can't get it," he said in a whisper. "Doesn't sound human. I don't like it!"

For a few moments the strange sound became louder; it was not a voice, but equally certainly it was not natural, and Scott gulped. There was something terrifying about it, and he felt cold and clammy. "It's evil," muttered Nigel, his face white. "I know it's evil —it's gone!"

The murmur stopped as suddenly as it had begun, and Vale breathed hard. "I felt it was evil, too," he said slowly, "but I can't tell you why. I'm not usually stupid enough to let my imagination take over, but—well, there it is."

"I'm sure of it," said Thor quietly.

Vale shrugged. "I don't know whether it's wise to keep the receiver full on, but we may all be making idiots of ourselves. We'd better keep a watch outside, I think. Thor, I'll need you to help with the circuits. There's only one chance that I can see, and it's the longest of long shots."

"I'll go out," said Scott. "I'll call up every minute or two. If you don't hear me, come out and haul me in."

Once again he went through the airlock, and once more he came out into that eerie blackness, totally un-lit by any star. For a moment he almost panicked. "I'm behaving like a kid," he thought angrily. "We'll get back somehow or other!" But as the minutes passed, the darkness began to get on his nerves, and it took all his resolution not to haul himself back into the airlock. Not that the ferry-rocket would be a safe home for long; its oxygen supplies were limited, and four people could hardly hope to survive for much more than a week. He called regularly, and Nigel answered, but then Vale's voice came through. "Scott!"

"Yes?"

"No sign of anything? It's starting to look bad," said

Vale, his voice unusually subdued. "I've one possible answer, but it means using more power than we've got on this confounded ferry. If only I'd had the common-sense to instal a separate drive unit, we might have stood a chance."

"What do you mean?" asked Scott.

"Quite simply, our only real hope is to use brute force," said Vale. "If I could concentrate enough power in one tremendous jolt, we might be blasted out of this alien universe back into our own. I'd hoped to make up the power by coupling the screen circuits on to our whole rocket propulsion unit, but even then we haven't enough. Better come inside, I think."

"Why? Doesn't seem to make much difference," muttered Scott.

"Not a great deal, I suppose. I'll go on trying," said Vale, "but I'm not going to make any promises. We seem to be in a kind of upside-down universe; time runs backwards, energy is reversed—if I had the equipment, there's nothing I'd like more than to make a proper study of it. Incredible!"

Nigel called out. "For Pete's sake come inside, pal. We'd better stick together."

"All right," said Scott. "Give me a few minutes, thought. There's always a chance that I'll spot something."

For what seemed hours he hung there, silent and in total darkness apart from the glow of the observation window. The starless sky was all around him; where was the sun—and above all, where was the earth where he had been born? Scott shivered. Perhaps for the first time, he realized how desperate their situation was. If they were isolated in an alien space-time, there was nothing that Sir Eustace or anyone else could do to help. Before long their oxygen would run out, and that would be the end.

Then, suddenly, he saw something, and gave a shout. "Nigel! Thor! Look out!"

"Where?" came Thor's voice.

"Over there—I can't show you, but it's on the far side of the observation window," said Scott breathlessly. "It's a light, and it's moving. Must be some kind of space-ship!"

A pause, and then Nigel came through. "I'm coming out," he said. "I'll bring all our flash signals. Whoever or whatever it is, we'd better tell him where we are. Right, Reggie?"

"Right," said Vale. "Thor, get on to the radio—full power. Do your best!"

Moments later, Nigel thrust through the airlock, carrying one of the powerful flashlights that had so often proved their value in space. "We'll keep on signalling," he said. "All we can do. Suppose—" he hesitated. "Suppose it really is something absolutely alien?"

"What's the odds?" asked Scott, twisting so as to keep the moving light in view. "I'd rather be beaten up by a bug-eyed monster than sit here waiting to choke. Look—it's getting brighter."

"You're right." Nigel swung the flash, and sent out a series of dots and dashes; no beam was visible in the emptiness of space, but with luck the light would be visible over a range of several miles. "It's closing in on us. Get set."

Steadily the light became plainer, until at last a dim shape could be made out. "Looks almost like a ferry," muttered Scott. "This is crazier than ever. It might be our own rocket . . . You don't think it can be 'us', do you?"

"How come?"

Scott stared into the starless blackness. "Well—if we're in a different space-time, there's always the chance that we're seeing a double of ourselves—in our own universe, I mean. Does that make sense, Reggie?"

"Nothing makes any sense at all. I'll come out," said Vale. "Keep the radio at maximum power, Thor, and let us know if you hear so much as a twitter. If that infernal murmur starts up again, I've a hunch that we may be in for trouble."

Scott was calm now, even though he was sweating inside his space-suit. Vale came through the airlock; still the light brightened, and at last there could be no doubt. It was a rocket very much like their own, and it was getting closer every second. Vale spoke sharply. "Thor, use the automatic homing beam; if we can get this thing really near in, we can have a look at it before we try to make contact. Switch off the protective screen. We're going to need every ounce of power we've got."

It was a tense few minutes, and Scott felt his heart thumping wildly. Who, or what, could be in this wandering space-ship? Would they find duplicates of themselves—or would they come face to face with a life-form so strange that they might not even recognize it? "Homing in," said Thor. "Any moment now."

The space-craft closed in, and Scott and Nigel could see the familiar shape of an observation window. Then there was a slight shudder, and the two rockets were left only a few feet apart, to all appearances motionless in space. Vale drew a deep breath. "We'll have to go in," he said. "The outer door isn't closed, so there can't be any air inside the cabin. That means that if it's been flown by people like us, they must be dead—"

"Unless they've kept their vacuum-suits on," said Nigel.

"Only one way to find out," said Scott, and eased himself forward, pulling on his safety-line. "Here goes."

Cautiously he eased his way into the airlock; once inside, he turned on the powerful light in his helmet, and gazed around. The inner door was loose, and he paused. "I'm inside. Wait," he said steadily, and pushed against the door. "It's—boy! This beats the lot!"

"What is it?" roared Vale.

Scott burst into a cracked laugh. "I told you this beats the lot. You know who's been flying this thing? It's Robbie, I tell you—it's Robbie!"

Chapter 10

INTO THE SUNLIGHT

Nigel let out a yell. "Robbie? You're joking!"

"Not on your life," said Scott, and thrust his way into the cabin. "He's here, as large as life, and I'm darned glad to see him. Hallo, Robbie!"

The robot turned. "I greet you," came the cold, metallic voice. "I greet you, friend."

Scott hesitated. "Have the orders been carried out?"

"Orders have been carried out. Mission successful."

"What happened after you fired the ray?"

This time there was no reply. "Too much for him," said Thor as he came through the airlock. "He hasn't been programmed to answer questions like that, and remember he can't think for himself. Robbie, were there any malfunctions?"

"No malfunctions. Orders have been carried out. Mission successful."

"A bit too successful, if you ask me," muttered Nigel. "He's well and truly blasted us out of our universe, even if it wasn't his fault. I'm glad he's come through, though, even though I don't see that he's going to be able to help us.

The headphones crackled. "Wrong," said Vale. "It's

116

just possible that there may be a way out of this mess after all. Thor, check over all the circuits in Robbie's rocket. If they're undamaged, I can try something that will either get us home or else blow us out of every universe that's ever existed."

"But—"

"Don't argue," rapped Vale. "Do as I tell you. Scott, you and Nigel may as well come back."

Scott half-turned. "What about Robbie?"

"No point in bringing him . . ." began Vale, and then broke off. "Confound it all, I'm getting sentimental in my old age. Get him across. We'll take him with us if we're going to get anywhere ourselves."

Scott gave a quick grin, and Nigel grinned back. True, Robbie was a machine, unable to think or feel, but if they had left him behind, to float forever in this black, lonely universe, they would have seemed like traitors. "Follow," said Scott, and Robbie replied: "I follow." As they went back through the airlock, Scott could not help giving an exclamation of alarm. Robbie had no need of a helmet or a vacuum-suit; all the same, it was uncanny to see a man-like figure moving unprotected in outer space.

Still there was no gleam of light except from the windows of the ferries, and the silence and desolation were complete. Nigel was just as affected as Scott, and as he looked around he gave a shudder. "Suppose we can't get back? Dying out here won't be much fun—"

"Stow it, pal," said Scott roughly. "We're not done yet. Let's hear what you've got in mind, Reggie."

Vale nodded, taking off his spectacles and polishing

them. "You know how we got here? The black hole may have been small, but when it exploded it was powerful enough to hurl us clean out of our own spacetime. At least, I imagine that's what happened."

"The black hole's gone, then?" said Nigel slowly.

"Gone from our universe, I think. When the energy-beam hit the lump of super-dense matter in the centre, the reaction was so violent that it crushed the material out of existence altogether. If so, then I'm prepared to bet that the black hole simply ceased to exist. There's been endless argument about that sort of thing, I know," added Vale thoughtfully. "I remember that absurd paper by Karl Müller—"

Scott managed a grim chuckle. "Pity your Mr. Müller isn't here now. I still don't get what you're trying to do."

"Couple up the circuits in our ferry, connect them with the power units of Robbie's rocket, and produce a concentrated force-field," said Vale bluntly. "It'll only last for about a thousandth of a second, but it may be enough to jerk us back where we belong. It'll be a once-only experiment, because it's bound to blow all the circuits and leave us without any reserves."

Nigel drew a deep breath. "Pretty scary, isn't it?"

Vale glared. "I'm not an imbecile. I know quite well that if this trick fails, we'll end up either in a great many little pieces or else quite helpless. Perhaps you'd rather do nothing, and stay here till our oxygen runs out?"

"Not on your life. You've got to give it a go," said Nigel in a low tone. "How long?"

"A few hours. It depends on how badly the other ferry has been damaged," said Vale. "Frankly, I can't imagine how it survived at all. By all the laws of scientific commonsense, it ought to have been torn to shreds by tidal forces the instant it passed over the event horizon . . . oh, well—no matter. I've got work to do, and so has Thor."

"What about us?"

"Nigel, keep a radio watch," said Vale. "There isn't a hope of Station One getting through, because they won't have any idea of what dimension we're in; for all I know, we may be occupying the same space in Universe No. Two as they are in Universe No. One. No, I'm unhappy about that murmuring we heard earlier. We all felt that it was evil, and I'm pretty sure we were right, though I can't tell you why." He paused. "Thor. What are the circuits like? If it means a major repair job, it may be too much for us."

"I can fix them," said Thor coolly. "Nothing wrong that can't be put right. It'll take an hour or two, but it's no problem."

"Thank heaven for that," said Vale, and Scott felt relieved; he knew that as an electronics "wizard", the Icelander was second only to Vale himself. Nigel went back to the radio desk, and settled down; Robbie remained standing upright, motionless and with his usual blank expression. "Good for you, old lad," said Scott, and bit back an exclamation as Robbie replied: "I thank you."

Scott wished that he had something definite to do. Vale and Thor were furiously busy, and Nigel concen-

119

trated on his radio watch; once or twice Scott spoke to Robbie, but by now he was starting to remember just what the robot could or could not do. "He'll be a better talker when we've cleared that last programme out of his brain," said Thor on one of the occasions when he came over from the second ferry. "He's only an experimental model, after all, and he's been pretty much overloaded."

"How are things going?"

"Not too bad. I've repaired the main power units in Robbie's rocket—luckily, there wasn't a lot wrong with them—and all we have to do now is to link them up with our own. Then we'll see how much power we've got."

"What are the chances?"

"Rather less than one in ten, if you must know," said Vale curtly. "It's a wild gamble, and I wouldn't be stupid enough to try it if I could think of anything better. Scott, I'll need your help in coupling the two ferries up. It's going to need some pretty clever piloting."

"Right," said Scott. "Let me know."

Suddenly Nigel let out a gasp, and raised his hand. "I can hear it again," he said softly. "Boy! I don't like it one little bit. Listen out."

Scott reached for his headphones, and plugged them in. Sure enough, he could hear something; far away there was that eerie, persistent murmur, wordless and filled with menace.

"All right. I can hear it," said Vale. "Get busy. I may be a nervous old fool, but I've a feeling that we may not have long to go. Bring the ferry in, Scott, and couple up the two airlocks while we work on the circuits."

Scott needed no urging, but all the time the murmur was growing louder, and he found it difficult to concentrate. "Stop it," he muttered angrily; he knew that he would need all his skill to manœuvre the two rockets until they could be linked, and it was only when he switched off his receiver that he could think clearly again.

Twice he tried, and twice he failed. All he could do was to use the tiny amount of power that Thor could spare; the motors of his own ferry were still dead. "It's not going to work," he panted. "Hang it all, we tried to fire our motors, and they wouldn't start up, so what good will it do?"

"Reggie's banking on using the whole lot in one almighty jolt," said Thor. "Don't tune in your receiver. I did, just now, and it made me dizzy right away."

Scott nodded, and made a third attempt. This time his calculations were perfect, and the two rockets clicked into position, but still there seemed to be something wrong. "I wish we hadn't heard that row," said Scott slowly. "Let's see if it's still there."

He switched on; at once his ears were filled with a loud murmur, and he felt his senses reeling. Hastily he switched off, and looked at Thor. "Better warn the others?"

"I guess so. Will you go in?"

Scott nodded, and thrust back through the airlock into the first ferry; by now the two space-craft were to all intents and purposes operating as a single unit. He came into the cabin, and then let out a shout. Both Nigel and Vale were there, but both were hanging limply clear of the floor, and for a ghastly moment Scott thought that they were dead. Frantically he wrenched off first Nigel's headphones and then Vale's; was he in time? Then, to his unutterable relief, Nigel's eyes flicked open. "Phew . . . my head. What was it?"

"Wish I knew. Reggie—wake up," said Scott urgently, and shook Vale roughly by the shoulder. "Reggie!"

"I'm—I'm all right. What an idiot," said Vale thickly. "I always had a feeling that that noise was dangerous, and I was right. Switch off Robbie's receiver, quickly. No knowing what devilish things may be going on. We may be just in time!"

"It's after us," said Nigel in a high-pitched voice, as Thor stumbled into the cabin. "My head. I—I can't tell you what it was like. It was ghastly!"

Vale shook himself. "Thor—start coupling up. Quick as you can. Stand by to help, Scott—put your vacuum-suits on, all of you, just in case we get badly knocked around. Hurry!"

Only Robbie remained unmoved as Scott went outside, and Vale and Thor worked furiously. "I'm starting to get the hang of it," said Nigel quietly. "Risk blowing the circuits—let them off in one big burst—but where will it land us? In our own universe, or somewhere else?"

"Don't know. Anything's better than staying here."

122

Nigel gave a shiver. "You've said it. Do you reckon this universe doesn't have any stars?"

"No sun either, so far as I can see. A universe of blackness," said Scott, and drew a deep breath. "It's—look! Nigel—look there!"

"Where?"

Scott raised an arm, and Nigel stared. "Sort of a glow. Not like the black hole—it's not like anything. I—I can't take my eyes away from it!"

Scott realized that he was unable to stir; his eyes were fixed on the distant glow, and try as he might he could not break free. He heard Nigel give a sobbing cry, and he fought with every ounce of his will-power; he almost fainted, but even without his receiver he could hear the wordless murmur rising to a scream. Suddenly he was wrenched round; the spell was broken, and he grabbed Nigel, pulling him away toward the airlock. "Close your eyes and get inside," roared Vale. "I'm going to chance everything!"

Scott panted. "What—what is it?"

"Never mind. Quickly!" Vale's voice rose. "Hang on to Robbie. He'll guide us."

Scott was clutching Nigel, his eyes tightly shut; he knew that if he looked back at that hellish light there would be no hope left. He felt a metallic clasp round his waist, and then he realized that he was inside the ferry. "No time to check," said Vale in a choked voice. "That sound! I can hear it even without the radio. I'm going mad!"

"You're not mad. It's something we can't understand. Reggie, where's the control?"

Vale pointed, and raised his arm. "Master switch. I can't get to it. I can't move—"

Scott's senses were reeling. The murmur was a shrill roar now, and the whole cabin was dancing and flickering; there was no physical movement—it was as though light itself was being whirled around. Nigel and Thor were silent and motionless; Vale struggled feebly, and every moment the menacing sound grew louder. Scott tried to move, but his muscles would not respond. Then, almost automatically, he gave a shout. "Robbie. Operate the master switch!"

Dimly, as the cabin reeled round, he could make out the metallic figure of the robot moving slowly but steadily toward the control panel. Then, as Scott watched, Robbie raised his metal arm; for an instant it hovered, and then fell full upon the vital switch. There was a flash—a scream—and a blaze of light; the robot was hurled back, and Scott knew no more.

Hours later, it seemed, he came round to see Nigel's face looking down at him anxiously. "O.K., pal?" said Nigel, and Scott half-choked. "Boy, you only just got us out of that one. I knew what was happening, but I couldn't do a thing about it."

Scott managed to struggle up. "Robbie did it. He was the only one of us who could beat that devilish thing. Where—where are we?"

"Look," said Vale, and pointed to the observation window. "The sun—and the earth. We're back in our own space-time, and I've no doubt that we'll be contacted by radar any time now."

"It worked, then?"

"It worked," said Vale, "though I can't pretend to understand all the details of it. What I did was to concentrate all our power in one particular region, just outside the ferry. That was enough to—well, to bend space and time, if you like, and jerk us back through the barrier . . . If I hadn't seen it myself, nothing would ever make me believe it."

"I don't think I believe it even now," said Nigel shakily. "Did we dream it? And what about the black hole?"

Vale gave a wry grin. "Confound it all, I'd almost forgotten. Until we get the radio working we can't call up, and I don't think any of our power-units can have survived the beating we gave them. We'll have to wait."

Actually it was only an hour or so later that Vale and Thor between them managed to make a temporary repair to the remaining power supplies. "Try," said Vale, and Nigel obeyed. The television screen glowed; for a few moments it flashed, and then, suddenly, a familiar face appeared. "Well, well, well," said Sir Eustace. "I thought I'd seen everything, but I'm bound to say that this little effort has left me speechless. Forgive my curiosity, but where exactly have you been? A quick flip to the Milky Way, or somewhere more exotic, such as Bognor Regis?"

"I don't know, but we're darned glad to be back," said Scott, as all four crowded round the screen. "Robbie pulled us out of it—"

"Robbie? At the moment I don't think my feeble brain will stand any more shocks," said Sir Eustace, "so if you don't mind we'll save the details until you get home. I may say that we know exactly where you are, and a ferry will be out to you in no time at all; it's on its way now. The sight of you popping up out of a trap is something that will haunt me for the rest of my days, but I admit that I've never been so relieved in my life."

"Basil—" began Scott.

"Basil the Black Hole has faded out, I'm delighted to tell you," said Sir Eustace. "There was a sort of flicker, and—well, he was no more. You can imagine how I felt when I thought you'd gone too," he added quietly. "What can I say except 'Thank you'? That's what the whole world will be saying."

"Thank Robbie," said Scott with a grin, and gave the metal robot an affectionate pat. "One thing's certain. He's not going to be taken to bits—he's a pal."

"Oddly enough," said Vale, "I feel the same way. I wonder what would have happened if we hadn't got free? It's beyond belief, but I don't suppose we'll ever find out."

Scott, Nigel and Thor made no reply. Then Scott turned back to the transparent window. It was no longer a scene of black loneliness. They were back in their own universe, and Scott knew that he had never been so glad to see the sun.

Have you read the first five books in the Scott Saunders Space Adventure Series by Patrick Moore?

SPY IN SPACE shoots Scott straight into a dramatic adventure as he leaves his home planet to study under the team of brilliant scientists on Space Station One – but it's not long before he discovers that one of his colleagues is a deadly traitor . . .

In **PLANET OF FEAR,** Scott and his friend Nigel Lorrimer go to rescue an exploratory team who crash-land on a strange planet, and find themselves plunged into a life-or-death struggle as they, too, fall victims to the planet's terrifying power . . .

In **THE MOON RAIDERS,** scientists at Lunar Base Three, on the far side of the Moon, are suspected of inventing a lethal 'death-ray' that could destroy the Earth. Scott is sent to investigate – and discovers the terrifying truth . . .

KILLER COMET is the gripping adventure of contamination in space from a dangerous comet. Nigel Lorrimer, testing the comet gas on board a satellite, is poisoned by the deadly fumes. He is surely doomed, Scott blasts off in a do-or-die rescue attempt – but will he get there in time?

In **TERROR STAR,** Scott and his friends on Space Station One receive weird messages from outer space. They come from a distant star, but one so terrible that it seems no one will escape its deadly power . . .

Armada

CAPTAIN ARMADA

has a whole shipload of exciting books for you

Here are just some of the best-selling titles that Armada has to offer:

⊐ **The Great Airport Mystery** Franklin W. Dixon 75p

⊐ **Killer Comet** Patrick Moore 50p

⊐ **Biggles in the Antarctic** Captain W. E. Johns 75p

⊐ **The Secret of the Golden Pavilion** Carolyn Keene 75p

⊐ **Saucers Over the Moor** Malcolm Saville 75p

⊐ **The Screaming Skull and Other True Mysteries** Peter Haining 60p

⊐ **SF2** Richard Davis 70p

⊐ **The Mystery of the Dancing Devil** Alfred Hitchcock 75p

⊐ **The Mystery of the Stuttering Parrot** Alfred Hitchcock 75p

⊐ **The Rockingdown Mystery** Enid Blyton 75p

Armadas are available in bookshops and newsagents, but can also be ordered by post.

HOW TO ORDER
ARMADA BOOKS, Cash Sales Dept., GPO Box 29, Douglas, Isle of Man, British Isles. Please send purchase price of book plus postage, as follows:—

      1—4 Books .... 10p per copy

      5 Books or more .... no further charge

      25 Books sent post free within U.K.

Overseas Customers: 12p per copy

NAME (Block letters) .

ADDRESS